Second Chance Love

by
Pamela S. Meyers

Bling!
Romance
Lighthouse Publishing of the Carolinas

SECOND CHANCE LOVE BY PAMELA S. MEYERS
Published by Bling! Romance
an imprint of Lighthouse Publishing of the Carolinas
2333 Barton Oaks Dr., Raleigh, NC 27614

ISBN: 978-1-946016-04-1
Copyright © 2017 by Pamela S. Meyers
Cover design by Elaina Lee
Interior design by Karthick Srinivasan

Available in print from your local bookstore, online, or from the publisher at:
lpcbooks.com

For more information on this book and the author, visit: http://pamelasmeyers.com

Brought to you by the creative team at Lighthouse Publishing of the Carolinas:
Marisa Deshaies, Managing Editor
Connie Troyer, General Editor
Judah Raine, Proofreader
Jennifer Leo, Proofreader

Library of Congress Cataloging-in-Publication Data
Meyers, Pamela S.
Second-Chance Love / Pamela S. Meyers 1st ed.

Printed in the United States of America.

PRAISE FOR *SECOND CHANCE LOVE*

When a city girl taking a risk on love feels as dangerous as a cowboy climbing onto a bull, readers are in for a boot-stomping adventure. *Second Chance Love* is packed full of honest emotion, a behind-the-scenes glimpse at rodeo life, and a front-row seat to a very sweet romance. Don't miss your chance to saddle up for this romantic ride.

~**Candee Fick,**
Author of *Catch of a Lifetime*
and *Dance Over Me*

Second Chance Love is a fun, easy-reading journey of hope as Jace and Sydney work their way past doubts and second-guesses to find forgiveness, trust and love. The characters are down-to-earth, with relatable flaws and fears, and the reader can't help rooting for them from page one. With likable characters, seamless storytelling, and just the right dose of rodeo flavor, this novel is an uplifting story that reminds you to never give up on the things—or the ones—you've always loved.

~**Emily C. Reynolds**
Author of *Picture Perfect*

With irresistible characters and plenty of heart, Pamela Meyers' *Second Chance Love* is definitely worth taking a chance on! This love story hooks you from the beginning and keeps you engaged. Meyers' gift for writing romance shines on every page.

~**Brandy Bruce**
Author of *Looks Like Love* and
the Romano Family series

Pamela Meyers's story drew me in and didn't let me go. Pam has experienced the rodeo as a frequent attender, and her details of the sport are impressive. Who can resist a cowboy and a rodeo? This book's a keeper!

~**Andrea Boeshaar**
Author of *Too Deep for Words*
and *Lily's Dilemma*

ACKNOWLEDGMENTS

Sometime in my childhood I sensed a need to write things down and began keeping a diary. At about the same time, I fell in love with all things cowboy and yearned to have a horse. But on my dad's salary there wasn't money for this small-town girl to have a horse of her own. Therefore, I gratified my wishes by watching cowboy shows on TV and reading books about cowboys and horses.

I didn't realize it then, but that need to write was the beginning of a calling from God. As an adult I wrote some free-verse poems and journaled. Later, I became editor of my church singles' group newsletter. It wasn't until I returned to college to get my degree in an accelerated adult program that I came to realize that God's calling included writing for publication.

I'm blessed to say that this will be my fourth published book and my first with Lighthouse Publishing of the Carolinas' Bling! imprint.

I am very fortunate to be working with such an exceptional team at Bling! Thank you, Sandie Bricker, for the faith you had in my writing despite some plot problems. Marisa Deshaies, you have been an exceptional managing editor—always available when needed and a great encourager. Connie Troyer, I have been blessed for the second time to have you as my content and line editor. Thank you for your eye to detail and the skills to find plot problems and provide workable solutions. Your exceptional ability to remember details mentioned chapters earlier and to note when they don't coincide with details mentioned later is so appreciated. I don't know how you do that!

Ed Crowder, thank you for being such a dear friend and for introducing me to rodeo and bull riding over a decade ago, reigniting that girlhood love of all things cowboy. Thanks for your willingness to answer my questions about bull riding and rodeo and for the encouragement you've given me with this story and all my writing.

Thank you, Kym McNabney, for critiquing a rough draft of the story. Your willingness to give of your time and share your thoughts on what you liked about the story as well as what didn't "add up" was so helpful and appreciated.

I will forever be grateful to my church life group: Betty, Judy, Jane, Sue, and Catherine for your interest in my writing and for your unceasing prayer support. I love you all. At times you stood in the gap by praying for this story to find a home and at other times you joined me in praising God for the blessings.

Last but not least, I am very grateful to the bull riders of the Professional Bull Riders (PBR) for providing me insight about the sport, including videos on how to ride a bull. Also, thanks to the Pioneer City Rodeo in Palestine, IL, for providing me with the perfect setting for this story. You put on a great PRCA-sanctioned rodeo. I've attended the rodeo every Labor Day weekend for over a ten years and it's one of the highlights of my year. Every time I finished writing a chapter in this book, I felt as if I'd actually been to the rodeo and couldn't wait for Labor Day to roll around so I could really be there again.

Much of what I include in this story setting is real, but I did fictionalize the hotel name, how the kids' clinic is run, and also the interior of the hospital. The Will Rogers State Park in Vincennes, IN, the Back Porch Smokehouse, and the Wabash Coffee House are all real and well worth your time, should you visit the area.

Reader, I hope in reading *Second Chance Love*, the truth of what Sydney had to learn about trusting God and not giving in to the fear of the unknown resonated with you. If you feel a sense of God's calling on your life to something you've never done or considered, pray about it, then turn it over to God. He will allow whatever is in His will for your life. That's something I had to learn myself and what Sydney had to learn too.

Until next time,

Pam

In memory of the late Sandie Bricker, who believed in me enough to acquire this book for my publisher despite the revisions it needed. She may be in heaven now, but a part of her remains in these pages. And for that I'm grateful.

1

Early September

Sydney Knight picked up the note from her boss and smiled. Harry Brownlee's ASAPs were never as urgent as they sounded. He probably had another unglamorous job for her. She'd intended to ask for a meeting that morning anyway, and now she wouldn't have to.

It was time for her late father's law partner to see her as more than Jim Knight's little girl—more like the thirty-year-old attorney she had become. Wasn't three years of grunt work long enough?

Sydney picked up the case file she'd grabbed yesterday before Harry'd had a chance to turn it down. This one had her name written all over it.

She made the short trip through the Brownlee and Associates' law offices and smiled at Harry's redheaded administrative assistant as she approached the woman's desk.

"Go on in, Sydney. He's waiting for you."

"Thanks, Ginger." Sydney knocked softly on Harry's door, opened it, and stepped inside. She shut the door and moved farther into the large office before addressing her boss. "I know you aren't in favor of us taking on too many pro-bono cases, but, honestly, Harry, I have to do this one. It's a special-needs child and—"

"Right now, *I* have a special need," he interrupted. "My nephew needs some common sense knocked into his head." Harry pushed a brown file folder across his massive desk in the direction of one of the visitor's chairs that faced him.

Uh-oh. This could mean trouble. Her boss had only one nephew that she knew of. Sydney crossed the spacious office and settled into the chair in front of the folder. As she reached for it, a black Stetson sitting on the other side of the desk caught her eye. She dropped her hand into her lap. Nephew *and* Stetson meant only one thing: *Jace McGowan.* "Okay, Harry, what's going on?"

He faced the wall of windows behind his chair. "Beautiful day. Not even a whitecap on the lake; lots of people already down there looking at the Bean. Never could figure out why that sculpture gets so much attention." He spun around and looked her in the eyes. "You were so helpful the last time Jace was in

Chicago, taking him around the city. I don't get it. He has a college degree and does a great job at riding bulls, but he lacks—"

Behind her, the door clicked open. She turned. Her gaze fell on cowboy boots the color of polished mahogany, then lifted to take in the long jeans-clad legs and broad shoulders straining at the seams of a crisp red-plaid shirt. The five-o'clock shadow was new but appealing.

Dark blue eyes peered at her as the right corner of his mouth lifted into the heart-stopping grin she remembered so well. "Syd, good to see you again." He looked past her shoulder and squinted with one eye at his uncle. "Uncle Harry didn't say to expect you here when I finished my phone call." He closed the space between them and sat in the matching visitor's chair to Sydney's left.

She willed her racing heart to slow and hoped she hadn't lost her voice with the magnetic pull of his eyes. "He didn't tell me to expect you either. Except the hat gave you away." She faced her boss, who wore a self-satisfied smirk. Hadn't Harry gotten the message that she and his drop-dead-gorgeous nephew were mismatched? Jace's reputation as a player was all she needed to put him on her most-unwanted list. Not to mention that he'd have to have a faith like hers. She'd learned her lesson after she'd eased up on that checklist she used to keep when her former fiancé hadn't met the faith requirement and bailed on what was to be their wedding day.

Harry stroked his impeccably trimmed beard, a mannerism he often used while scrambling for the right words. "How long ago was it that you two took a tour of the city together? Two years? Three?"

Two, but who's counting?

Her boss looked from Jace to her, then back to his nephew. "Like I mentioned to you earlier, Jace, I need to be in court. I didn't have time to tell Sydney about your contract issues. She knows her stuff, and I'm sure she can give you solid advice about the dispute. I've made reservations at Lou Malnati's over on State Street. Your favorite."

"There's no need for that, Uncle Harry." Jace squirmed in his seat.

Sydney relaxed. Good. He didn't want to spend his lunch hour with her any more than she did with him. They could resolve the whole thing right now. That was much better than sharing a meal—too much like a date.

"But I'll gladly accept a Malnati's deep dish, and being able to catch up with Syd is a bonus." He glanced at Sydney and winked.

Heat warmed her cheeks, and she stared at her lap.

"They have a gluten-free veggie pizza."

"I know Malnati's menu, Harry." Sydney picked up the brown folder from where it lay on the desk. "What contract dispute?"

"Jace can explain it over lunch."

Leaving the file she'd brought with her on her lap, she flipped open the file from the desk, then scanned the contract and Harry's highlighted paragraphs that referred to penalties of early cancellation. Frisky's Restaurant chain was not a strong example of moral restraint on Jace's part. If she weren't already bogged down with other tedious work, she'd volunteer her time to educate women about being used as sex objects.

She shut the folder. Whatever Jace's issue was, she'd have it settled by the time he finished his deep dish. "It's only a short walk. We may as well beat the lunch crowd." Sydney stood, and the case file she'd brought with her tumbled from her lap. Leave it to the cowboy to distract her, just as he had last time.

She bent and reached for the folder and the papers that peeked out. Jace's large hand covered hers as his gaze collided with her startled one.

Shivers tingled up her arm.

"I was fixin' to get that for you, Sydney."

Her breath hitched and she nodded.

"You'll have to remove your hand."

Maybe she could stop at the drugstore on the way for earplugs to block the Texas accent that made everything he said sound like a beautiful sonnet. "Right." She lifted her hand and stood, certain the blush she'd felt earlier had crept down her neck. Acting like a lovesick schoolgirl over a man she'd spent only twelve hours with two years ago was not professional. She needed to get a grip.

Jace handed her the file and his features hardened. "I'm happy to have lunch with you, Syd, but I'm not going to change my mind. I'm done with Frisky's."

She gathered the file she'd brought from her office along with Jace's. "I'll get my purse. You can fill me in as we walk."

Jace opened the door to the street and Sydney marched past him. Her flowery scent lifted on the breeze and assaulted his senses. The same perfume that had nearly intoxicated him two years ago.

I'm in trouble.

If he'd known his uncle would involve Sydney in what he thought was a family discussion, he'd have declined Mom's suggestion to visit his uncle and said he had to be in Wisconsin.

He followed her out onto the sidewalk, and she looked at him. "It's about an eight-block walk. Is that okay with you? I try to walk everywhere I can, for the exercise."

He glanced at her red shoes. The heels had to be at least four inches high. "Sounds good to me."

Letting Syd lead the way down the crowded sidewalk, he planted himself next to her, with Michigan Avenue and Millennium Park to his left. He jammed his hands into his jeans pockets and looked off past the park toward the lake. The last time they were together, they'd talked nonstop. Today, he felt like a schoolboy on his first date. Someone had to break the ice. "So how have you been the past two years?"

She glanced his direction and picked up her pace. "Fine. Working hard, and that's about it. What about you?"

"Can't complain. Ridin' bulls, raisin' bulls, and tendin' the ranch. You're looking good. Life must be treating you well despite the daily grind."

"When you have a job you love, it never seems like work."

He frowned and stared at the concrete as he walked. Nice deflect. The woman probably had guys asking her out every night of the week. Or maybe by now she had a significant other. "Looks to me like you're still being assigned 'trench work,' as you called your job last time we were together. I figured, by now, you'd be trying those cases you were aspiring to oversee, not counseling the boss's rebellious nephew."

She huffed a laugh. "I'm happy to help out your uncle since his schedule's jammed. I'm working on cases—doing discovery. The courtroom assignments should come very soon."

He resisted asking what "discovery" was. Enough talk about the law. "And what occupies your time on weekends?"

She crossed her arms, causing her briefcase to swing on its shoulder strap. Her full red lips pressed together.

He got the message, and a disappointing one at that. The attraction she'd felt for him two years ago no longer existed. "Sorry if I ask too many questions. Just wanted to make conversation."

They reached an intersection as a taxi squealed around the corner. Sydney faced him, and her large brown eyes, framed by the longest lashes he'd ever seen, searched his face. "I'm sorry, Jace. This is to be a business lunch, and if we can discuss your contract issues as we walk, we'll be on our separate ways all the sooner. I'm only trying to keep our agreement. Or have you forgotten?"

How could he forget agreeing that despite falling hard for each other that long-ago day, they weren't a good fit? Not with her legal work in Chicago and him being tied up with the family ranch. "I haven't forgotten, but it doesn't mean we can't enjoy each other's company. I'm not interested in anything beyond that and appeasing Uncle Harry, who, I'm sure, is trying to appease my mom." Did he really mean those words? He may have felt that way two years ago, but not now. Especially the way his feelings for her so suddenly returned the moment he saw her sitting in Uncle Harry's office. He needed to show her as soon as possible that he was a changed man.

A shadow of disappointment appeared in her eyes. She glanced across the street. "Let's hurry and make this light before it goes red. The restaurant is only a couple more blocks away." Syd raised her chin and crossed the street with a determined expression.

If she walked any faster, Jace would have to jog to keep up. The only sounds filling his ears the rest of the walk were honking horns and the clacking of her red high heels hitting the pavement. So much for the business conversation she wanted to start. By the time they arrived at Malnati's, two streets away, Jace wondered if they shouldn't ditch the pizza, grab lunch from the food truck parked across the way, and head to the park for a chat—a much better place for conversation than inside the noisy restaurant. A place that would give him an opportunity to share about his changed way of life.

"Jace, wait here a sec."

Sydney scurried across the street and approached the food truck, which was decorated with a huge picture of a sub sandwich. A minute later, she emerged from the far side of the truck with a white sack and a paper cup in hand. She scurried back across the street to a man seated on the sidewalk in front of a 7-Eleven window next door to Malnati's.

The man's scruffy beard, worn work pants, and tattered Chicago Cubs T-shirt contrasted with the business attire of the people rushing past him. He stopped playing his harmonica and offered a toothless grin as Syd handed him the bag and drink. "Enjoy your lunch. God bless you."

A gap-toothed grin split his face. "No, God bless you, lady."

Jace's heart swelled as Sydney approached him. "That was nice of you. As close as I was to him, I never noticed the guy, even with his playing the harmonica."

"Please, no accolades. You'd have done the same if you'd seen him."

"I'm not sure about that. I don't run into homeless people much on the ranch, and I don't get into downtown San Antonio often except to see my attorney." They stepped up to the restaurant's entrance, and Jace pulled the door open. The aroma of garlic and oregano teased his nose, setting off a rumble in his stomach. He'd order an extra-large deep dish and have the leftovers boxed up. If the homeless man had moved on, he'd watch for someone else to give it to. God had changed him a lot in the past year, and he still had a ways to go.

2

Jace waited while Sydney informed the hostess of their reservation, then trailed behind her as they were led to a booth. Her shoulder-length waves, the color of light honey, bounced in time with the sway of her hips. The one time he'd embraced her on that long-ago night and felt those waves as they'd brushed his hand intruded on his thoughts. He forced his musings elsewhere. He didn't need a woman who was married to her job and craved city life. His future wife had to love ranch living and horses, because he wasn't going anywhere else. Not only that, but he needed someone who shared his faith. Something he was only beginning to understand.

Jace waited for Syd to sit, then slid onto the cushioned bench across from her. He dropped his Stetson onto the seat and glanced at the colorful menu the hostess left. A moment later, he pushed it aside. "I already know what I want. An extra-large Chicago Classic. That okay with you?"

"Order whatever you like." Sydney spoke without looking up from the menu. "I'm having a salad." She dropped her menu on top of his.

"That's all?" Their gazes connected. The sudden vulnerability in her eyes caught him off guard. "You sure a salad will hold you all afternoon?"

"I don't need a large lunch." A hint of a smile tipped the corners of her full lips. "Are you really planning to eat an extra-large deep dish all by yourself?"

A guy could drown in her smile. For a moment Jace wasn't hungry at all. Then he blinked. "I don't plan on eating all of it. Thought maybe the man out there you fed would like to share a little of the best pizza on earth with us."

Her eyes widened. "Don't feel you have to do that because of what I did."

"Wouldn't think of it. Is that okay with you?"

"Yes, of course. You do realize Harry is paying for the lunch."

"Figured so. I'll toss in the cost of the pizza."

"No, let Harry spring for it. I'll tell him later."

Jace shrugged. "Fine by me." He opened the menu and studied it. "The sausage on their special is the absolute best I've tasted. I'm willing to get the gluten-free dough. If you're a pepperoni gal..." The curious expression on her face made him laugh. "I was just testing you. I know you're a vegetarian."

"Not vegetarian or gluten-intolerant. Harry gets confused. But I do avoid eating red meat." She kept her eyes fixed on him as if waiting for a reaction.

His memory cleared. Two years ago, they'd laughed at the irony that he raised cattle for the very food she avoided. Jace picked up his silverware pack and unrolled it, then placed the knife and fork on the polished wood table. He spread the napkin on his lap before looking up into those dark eyes. "How about we make it half cheese and spinach and half the Chicago Classic?"

"I've been good this week. The spinach and cheese is too delicious to pass up."

He grinned and felt the tension leave his shoulders. "Great. Let's get the grub ordered so we can get our business discussed and enjoy the meal."

After the waiter took their order, Jace leaned back in the booth. Sydney had pulled out her iPhone and was scrolling through what he presumed was her e-mail. The tiny crease between her eyes and the way her lips pursed as she read fascinated him.

She finished tapping out a message, then slipped the cell phone into her bag and ran her gaze over him. Was it disappointment he saw in her eyes—for what they had both wanted but couldn't have? At least according to *her* they couldn't have. Had it taken her as long to get over him as it did him to move on? Maybe he'd find out before this lunch was over.

Sydney opened Jace's file and reread Harry's sticky note, which explained why Jace needed some common sense. An uneasy sensation that she was being watched came over her, and she looked up. Jace kept his gaze pinned on her, not seeming to care that she'd caught him in the act. "How long have you been watching me?"

He chuckled. "Long enough to wonder when you were going to notice. That must be some interesting file."

"I didn't know bull riders had sponsors."

"Most professional bull riders have sponsors. I agreed to wear Frisky's logo on my shirt, do promotional appearances at their restaurants, and pose with their wait staff. In return, they pay me the generous sum noted on the contract, which helps me get from one successful bull ride to the next."

"Like race car drivers."

His eyes lit up. "Yeah, like them."

She skimmed the agreement. No one in his right mind would walk away from any contract without negotiating a settlement. "It looks like you have two more years on the agreement. Why not just wait it out?"

Jace rested his elbows on the table and leaned toward her. "Almost a year and a half ago, I surrendered my life to God ... and everything changed. As much as I tried to fulfill my agreement to be at their events and have pictures taken with the waitresses in those skimpy outfits, I couldn't do it anymore. It's not what God wants me to be doing—which is setting a good example." He sat back, never taking his penetrating stare away from her.

Sydney pushed out a smile and mentally thanked God for Jace's new faith. "Jace, that's wonderful news." She opened her purse and jammed her hand inside, a motion to buy time to process what he'd said. With his Christian testimony, she'd just lost the best argument for not having a relationship with him. At least an argument that would make sense to most of her friends. Her hand landed on a container of peppermints, and she pulled the tin from her purse and waited for the server to serve their drinks. "Personally, I've never cared for Frisky's over-the-top fixation on women, and I admire your courage to stand up for your beliefs. Unfortunately, what you believe now has no bearing on what you agreed to in the contract." She opened the tin of mints and held it out to Jace.

He shook his head, then his eyes creased at the corners and the twinkle returned to his baby blues. "Then you agree with me about God and Frisky's?"

"Yes." She selected a mint, slipped it into her mouth, and returned the tin to her purse. *Time to change the subject.* "Have you already spoken to Frisky's about this?"

"Yep. No deal."

"I haven't had time to read the entire document, but from what Harry has highlighted, the contract looks very tight. I'm surprised your attorney didn't negotiate a better deal."

Jace rested his elbow on the table and used his cupped hand for a chin rest. He let his gaze settle on her. "How long have you avoided red meat?"

"Since law school." She clenched her jaw and lifted her chin. "Did you hear what I just said?"

"I didn't use an attorney." He sat back and affected a relaxed pose. "Didn't think I'd need one. I'd already given my attorney enough work. Have you had a steak or burger since you stopped?"

She rubbed the back of her neck. The man was hopeless. "Once or twice. I advise you to never sign anything again without legal counsel. You could lose a lot of money by breaking this contract early."

"I know. Did you enjoy it?"

She sighed and worked to stifle a giggle burbling in her throat. "Enjoy what?" Risky question. Every good attorney knew to never ask a question unless they already knew the answer.

"Meat ... when you ate it."

"Jace McGowan. This is no joke." She leaned across the table and narrowed her eyes. "If you break this contract without negotiation, your sponsor has every right to clean out your bank account, and there's nothing you can do about it. I agree that you should dissolve the contract as soon as possible, but the way you're going about it is only inviting costly legal trouble. The key word here is *renegotiation*."

His smile dissolved. He picked up his glass of Dr Pepper. "Look, can we say you've done your best to convince me and be done with it? They've already told me they won't budge, and there isn't any way I can do that kind of promotion and acknowledge my relationship with God at the same time. As far as I'm concerned, the association with Frisky's is over."

"Can you afford the $150,000 fine you'll have to pay?"

His shoulders dropped ever so slightly. "To be honest, no. My dad died almost two years ago and surprised us all with a tax lien on the ranch. He was trying to pay it down, but cancer got the best of him. Every penny I win goes toward the taxes—after ranch expenses, of course."

Her heart ached to forget the reason for the meeting and offer comfort. Harry should have prepared her better. "Is bull riding your only income?" *How can anyone make a living that way?*

"No. We have a large herd of cattle, and we're in the black with that operation, but the margin is thin. I've started a stock-contracting business, raising bulls to buck. In time, that will help a lot."

Their waiter approached, carrying a round silver pan with their pizza. He set a rack in the center of the table and placed the steaming deep dish on top. Already, the sausage aroma from Jace's half mingling with the onion and garlic on her portion set her stomach to growling. While the server cut their slices and served them, Jace crossed his arms and kept his gaze fixed on Sydney. She grabbed the stand-up card on the table and studied the colorful photo of a chocolate brownie sundae.

The server left and Sydney looked up. Jace had bowed his head and closed his eyes. She did the same. She'd let him pray for the food. She needed God's strength to resist his charm.

Sydney raised her head and their eyes met. His twinkled with joy, while hers, she was certain, held both the elation and the dread she'd been feeling for the past fifteen minutes.

He spoke first. "My bad. I should have asked if you wanted to say the blessing together. I'm so used to being around people who don't believe that I forget to ask."

She shrugged. "I usually pray silently before a meal. I'm used to it."

Jace sliced his fork through the tip of the pie-shaped wedge and brought the morsel to his mouth. He closed his lips around the forkful and shut his eyes as an expression of bliss appeared on his face.

A sudden desire to taste what was causing him to almost swoon came over her. The ex-fiancé who'd convinced her to stop eating red meat may have long ago exited her life when he went back to his former girlfriend, but not eating beef was the last vestige of Ryan she held on to—kept for health reasons only. But one tiny taste couldn't hurt.... She gave herself a mental shake and picked up her fork. If she was going to break down and eat red meat, she should at least do it with a steak. She dove into her veggie slice, happy for the silence while they ate.

Long after Sydney had eaten her fill, Jace set down his fork and took a swig of his drink. "I can't eat another bite."

"I can't either."

Jace eyed her plate. "You didn't finish your first slice."

"I ate everything except the crust." She pushed the plate to the side and kept her expression serious. "I'm sorry to hear about your father passing away."

He took a deep breath and exhaled. "Thanks. That's what triggered turning my life over to God. Dad lived only a month after he was diagnosed."

She offered a weak smile. "And the ranch responsibility all fell on you. How much help do you have?"

"I have a couple of guys who work the ranch with me seasonally, along with my younger twin brothers, who are in high school. My buddy, Clint, also lives on the ranch and helps with the stock-contracting business and other chores when we're not doing rodeos. He's a bullfighter."

An image of a Spanish bullfighter waving a red cloth in front of an angry bull popped into Sydney's thoughts. "Rodeos have a bullfighting event too?"

He grinned and shook his head. "Not the kind most people would think of. Bull riding needs two or three guys called *bullfighters* to distract the bulls after their riders come off. Once the riders are safe, the bulls are herded back to the pens."

"Sounds dangerous."

"It can be, but bullfighters are very skilled and there are few accidents."

"You mentioned before about raising bulls and called it a stock-contracting business. What exactly does that mean?"

He straightened. "Just about the best deal around for a retired bull rider. Most rodeos and bull-riding events use stock contractors to supply the animals. I raise bulls and train them to buck. This year I started supplying them to rodeos. It can be a very good living."

She felt her eyes widen. "I never realized how much went into bull riding. And all this came about since your father passed." Moisture pooled in her eyes, and she blinked it away. "There's nothing good about losing a parent."

Jace picked up his glass and swirled the ice cubes with a wrist movement. "Sounds like you've gone through the same thing."

A familiar heaviness came over her like a fog. *Best to make the facts short and sweet and change the subject.* "My dad died when I was sixteen. It's not something I talk about much."

"Cancer too?"

"Accident." She reached for the folder and opened it. "You really should have had an attorney help with this contract. It makes no provision for renegotiation if either party wants to make amendments."

"The wording seemed so simple, and I had no problem with what they wanted me to do. Now, with all that's changed in my life, it wasn't such a good idea." He paused. "What else can I do when God doesn't condone the message Frisky's sends out?"

"I know, but God also expects us to use the brains He gave us. And He expects us to fulfill our promises. There's a right way to break a contract and a wrong way. Right now, you're doing it all wrong. Are you really equipped to cover the fine?"

"I can if I win big at the next two rodeos and make it to the NFR in December. If that doesn't work out, I'll have to sell a couple of bulls. But either way, I can't go against God."

Admiration for the man skyrocketed as that checklist of hers materialized in her thoughts. He'd just ticked the "admirable qualities" box. She shook off the thought and quirked her head. "The NFR?"

"National Finals Rodeo in Vegas during December. Lots of money to be won."

"Rodeos can't pay that much."

"You'd be surprised. And don't forget, I've got some bull stock in the game. This past Friday, we hauled my four- and five-year-olds to a rodeo in Wisconsin. Two bucked off their riders and got high scores. They're going to buck at the rodeo I'm entering this coming weekend too. In fact, I'm meeting Clint, my driver, over in Rockford later, and we'll head down to the rodeo arena in southern Illinois."

"Clint the bullfighter and ranch hand and driver. He's a multitalented guy. How do you haul the bulls?"

"There are all kinds of trailers we use on the ranch. For long hauling, I prefer one that has living quarters and enough room for the animals."

"I take it you're needing more than a pickup truck to haul something like that."

"Yep. It's a regular semi-cab like you see hauling eighteen-wheelers on the highway."

Her phone chimed from her purse. She excused herself and read Harry's text. Has he agreed yet?

She responded, then tossed the phone into her purse. "Sorry. What were you saying about a rodeo coming up?"

"After you and I finish lunch, I'll meet up with Clint, the man of many talents, in Rockford and head down to Palestine for their Labor Day–weekend rodeo. I need to be there a few days early to plan a rodeo clinic I'm giving for kids."

Fine, he works with kids. Another one of those boxes checked. An ache filled her chest as she shut the folder and slid it into her briefcase. "You have a full and interesting life." *Too bad I can't be a part of it.*

His robust laugh filled the air.

She offered a closed-mouth smile. "I'm not sure what's so funny."

He shook his head and grinned. "What you said about my life being full and interesting. At least we can end this discussion on a positive note." He tugged his cell phone from his pocket and looked at it. "Time for me to rock and roll and for you to get back to the office. Shall we get a box for the leftovers and look for Harmonica Man?"

She had forgotten all about the homeless guy. Two years ago, her feelings had been about Jace's charm and good looks. Today, he'd presented the whole package. And in a few more minutes, he'd be out of her life again. Maybe for good. If only she could stop listening to that taunting voice in her head, reminding her why life spent alone was for her own good.

"Syd, did you hear me?"

She startled. "Yes. It's time to go." She signaled the waiter for the bill. "I'll tell Harry you're as stubborn as those bulls you're crazy enough to ride—and raise."

"Bulls aren't as stubborn as you think."

She cast him a wary eye, then asked a busboy for a box for the leftovers. The faster they said their good-byes, the better.

The server appeared, placing a leatherette folder and a cardboard box in front of Jace. "Sorry it took so long."

Sydney reached across the table and grabbed the folder. "Why don't you take care of the pizza while I pay?" She tucked her business credit card inside the folder and handed it to the server.

Jace put the leftover pizza into the box and then received a text. Sydney sat staring at the relief map of Chicago affixed to the far wall, mentally spotting her work location and where her apartment in Wrigleyville was located, while he responded to his message.

"What are you staring at?" Jace twisted in his seat to look. "Hey, that's pretty cool."

Their server returned with the folder containing the receipt as they fell silent. After making sure the calculations were correct, she added a generous tip, signed on the line, and slipped her credit card into her purse. She looked up and was surprised to see Jace watching her again.

"I guess we're done. You need to meet your driver, and I have work to finish."

"Yep. You know the old saying—'All good things must come to an end.' " He smiled. "At least for me, this has been an enjoyable lunch." He slid out of the booth and picked up the box containing the pizza.

He was waiting for her to get up too. Good manners of a Southern gentlemen. She blocked thoughts of the checklist from her mind and slid out of the booth, relieved that he didn't appear to want her opinion about their time together. If he did, with her feelings teeter-tottering between pleasure and the need to escape, she wouldn't know what to say.

Outside, Jace set his Stetson on his head and looked down the sidewalk. "Good. He's still there. Come with me."

Sydney walked with Jace to the man, and Jace held out the box.

"We thought you should have some of the great pizza we just enjoyed."

The man glanced at Sydney, and recognition crossed his grizzled face.

She smiled and nodded.

The man gripped the box and looked up at Jace. "This sure is my lucky day. Thanks, cowboy."

Jace offered a crooked smile. "No, my friend, this is *my* lucky day. Enjoy." Without waiting for the man to respond, Jace touched Sydney's elbow. "Let's go."

Maybe they could say good-bye right there before she melted on the sidewalk. She could do this. Ten minutes more and she'd be back in her safe but boring life.

They walked toward the office in silence for several minutes.

"Syd, I'm sorry I couldn't take your advice about the contract."

"No problem. You have to do what you feel is right, even if it isn't the wisest move on the planet."

"Thanks for understanding."

"I never asked how you got here from O'Hare."

"I rented a car and will leave it in Rockford when I meet up with Clint."

They walked the rest of the way, making polite conversation, until they stopped in front of her building's door. Jace dropped his gaze to his boots. "I'd better get a move on. Good to see you again, Syd." He circled his arm around her waist and drew her to his side briefly, then let go. "Tell Uncle Harry thanks for lunch. Maybe we'll see each other the next time I pass through—do Malnati's again." He turned and headed down the street without looking back.

As much as the hug was more like the kind she gave to her platonic guy friends, she was relieved that it didn't last any longer than it had. She slipped through the door and crossed to the elevator bank.

After the cowboy had swooped in and out of her life two years ago, it had taken her at least three months to recover. Hopefully this time she was stronger. There could be no more "next time." Period.

By the time Jace neared Rockford, his meeting point with Clint, he'd rehearsed all the "what-ifs" that looped in his thoughts. What if he and Syd had tried to make a relationship work two years ago? What if today they'd picked up where they'd left off and agreed to give a long-distance relationship a go? What if he told Clint to go on ahead to the rodeo arena without him and he'd catch up in a couple days? Was the regret in Syd's eyes when they'd said good-bye a crack in her veneer? He'd agreed two years ago that they were mismatched, but now, knowing that she shared his faith, he wasn't as sure.

His cell phone rang. He pressed a button on his headset. "McGowan here."

"I saw Sydney a few minutes ago. I'm sorry she couldn't get you to change your mind."

"Hi, Uncle Harry. I told you I wouldn't budge. But Sydney tried real hard to convince me. Don't hold it against her."

"I'm sure she did. Too bad you had to leave so quickly. Maybe with another meeting..."

Jace drummed his fingers on the steering wheel. If Uncle Harry thought he could convince Jace to come back to Chicago after the weekend, he was wrong. As much as he wouldn't mind a few more minutes with one beautiful lawyer, the ranch was calling his name.

"Aren't you headed to that Labor Day–weekend rodeo downstate?"

Jace grinned. "Yeah. The Pioneer City Rodeo in Palestine."

"You mind if you have some company down there?"

He chuckled. Was he thinking Sydney? "As long as it's not you."

"Let me do some checking and I'll call you back."

3

The next morning, a note scrawled on Harry's personal notepaper sat in the middle of Sydney's empty desk. Her chest tightened, and she forced herself to take one breath and then another. She'd managed to overcome most of her OCD tendencies that began after her dad's death, but not having a perfectly clean desk unless she was working at it was the most difficult.

She snatched up the note and read.

SYDNEY, COME TO MY OFFICE AS SOON AS YOU GET IN!!!!

A large curlicue *H* filled the rest of the notepaper. Four exclamation points meant now, not later. She groaned and set her briefcase on the chair next to her desk. The last time Harry had left her a note like this, she'd ended up having lunch with Jace. But by now, the cowboy was in southern Illinois, far, far away. At least whatever Harry wanted wouldn't have anything to do with him.

With Jace's file to return in one hand and a latte in the other, Sydney scurried down the hall to Harry's office suite. She stepped past his administrative assistant's vacant desk and tapped on the polished wood door.

At Harry's "Come on in, Sydney," she opened the door and stepped inside the sun-splashed office.

Harry was leaning back in his leather chair with his Tom Ford wingtips propped up on his desk and his personal cell phone to his ear. He waved Sydney inside. "She's here now. What day did you say? ... Tomorrow night sounds good. I hope I can get her a hotel room."

Sydney smiled as she dropped into a visitor's chair. Harry must be sending her to Indiana to work on the case that was going to court next week. At least something was happening right.

Harry frowned. "No rooms anywhere? ... Is the place nice? ... Indiana? Okay, if that's all that's available. Get back to me as soon as you know something." He ended the call and looked at Sydney. His lips turned up at the corners.

She'd seen that fatherly smile many times since her dad died. It said he was about to say something she would like.

Sydney placed Jace's file on the desk and pushed it toward Harry. "I'm surprised there aren't any vacancies in Indianapolis. Is a large convention going on down there?"

He gave her a blank stare. "Indianapolis? Where'd you get that idea? I was talking about Robinson, Illinois, near where Jace is riding bulls this coming weekend." He pulled his feet off the desk and sat up.

A sinking sensation washed over her. "When you said Indiana, I thought you were talking about the new case. Are you and Joanne going downstate to watch Jace in the rodeo?"

"Are you kidding? The last place my wife would want to go is a rodeo. I'm sending you. My sister is really on me for letting him get away without assurance that he won't do something stupid." He leaned forward and grinned. "He'll listen to you before he does his old uncle. Leave work early today and start packing. You'll drive down tomorrow. He's there until Sunday morning."

Sydney managed a tight smile. How could a grown man let his sister push him around like that? She moved Harry's desk calendar over a couple of inches until it sat directly in the center, then picked up his sailboat paperweight and placed it several inches to the left.

Harry's hand covered hers before she could grab the pen-and-pencil set. "Sydney, stop. My desk is fine. What about this assignment is so troubling?"

Sydney sat back and forced down her need to move the pen set the inch it needed to line up with the other items. "How do you know I'm troubled?"

"Because you haven't taken to rearranging my desk since the time I sent you to our archive storage to put our files on the computer system—two years ago."

She let out a loud breath. "Mom and I always get together on Labor Day weekend. I don't know what she'll do if—"

"If you head to Palestine tomorrow, you can spend Thursday and Friday talking some sense into Jace and be home as early as Saturday afternoon. You'll have Sunday and Monday. Does your mom still need company every Labor Day?"

She picked a piece of lint from her skirt, then shifted her position. "You know Dad died on Labor Day weekend, and it's always been a troubling time for Mom and me. Or has it been so long that you don't remember?"

Harry frowned. "Of course I remember. How could I not? I lost my law partner and best friend that day. But it's been fourteen years, Syd. I'm sure your father would want you to move on."

"It still seems like yesterday."

"Are you sure this Labor Day ritual isn't more for you than for your mother? Joanne tells me that your mom's dating someone. Maybe she would, ah ... prefer spending the holiday with her new friend."

So now her mother was telling everyone about her new man. Last week, Mom couldn't stop giggling over some silly thing her new boyfriend had said.

When had Mom become the daughter and Sydney the mom? "They've only been friends for a month. Our Labor Day weekend has been carved in stone for thirteen years. I doubt it will be different this year."

"Do this for me, and maybe I could arrange for you to sit in on the Kolwalski case." Harry drummed his fingertips on the desk.

She squirmed. "Is this a joke?"

He flushed and offered a nervous laugh. "Why would I joke?" He drew in a breath and held it for a couple of moments. "I believe you are ready to be in a trial case. I was going to tell you after the holiday."

She didn't believe him for a minute, but she had Harry in a corner now. She'd been ready for months, and now he'd have to follow through. No rodeo or off-duty meals with the cowboy, though—too tempting to let her guard down. She was only going to see Jace to discuss the contract and then come home.

Jace watched the Illinois prairie slip past the passenger-side window, field after field of corn and soybeans. He glanced over at Clint Palmer, grateful that the man had insisted on driving, because Jace's mind was too unsettled to concentrate. He couldn't get his uncle's last words out of his mind. If Sydney came to the rodeo, he was asking for a peck of trouble. Yet he couldn't help wishing she would. Good thing he wasn't riding any bulls for a couple of days. If he were, he'd buck off in seconds.

"You look like your head is in another universe. What's with that?"

Jace glanced at Clint. His best buddy knew him well. "You don't want to know."

Clint chuckled. "It must be a woman. I know you didn't meet anybody up in Wisconsin, and you were only in Chicago for a few hours. She must be something to get your head all tangled up."

"Actually, it's someone I met two years ago. She works for my uncle." He tilted his head back and closed his eyes. He really didn't want to talk anymore. Clint never pried much, and hopefully he'd forget about what little they'd said.

Jace's phone rang. He pulled the device from his shirt pocket and checked the screen. His uncle's headshot stared back at him. He swiped the screen. "Hi, Uncle Harry."

"Sydney will be in Palestine tomorrow afternoon. She needs to leave no later than Sunday morning at the latest, but I told her she could likely leave Saturday, if you'll be reasonable and agree to renegotiate an end to the contract."

Syd is coming. Syd is coming.

"Jace, you still there?"

"Um, yeah, just got distracted."

"You're not driving, are you?"

"No. Clint is."

"Good. I need you to pull some strings and get her a room at one of those hotels in Robinson you mentioned. The Internet sites say they're full."

"I don't know how much weight I have. I'm only a peon."

"Well, try. I don't want her driving miles into Indiana."

Jace clicked off with his uncle a few moments later and then found the phone number for his hotel in Robinson, a small town minutes away from Palestine.

A friendly sounding woman answered. Yes, she remembered who he was from last year—the nice young man who preferred the Jacuzzi suite. If she could give him a room for his friend, she would, but a vacancy wasn't to be had until Monday. He declined her suggestion that his friend bunk with him and tried the other hotel down the street instead. It was booked up as well. All the clerk could offer was a suggestion to try hotels across the Wabash River in Indiana. But to get there, Syd would have to drive a good twenty to thirty minutes south or north to the nearest bridges. *Good-bye, Jacuzzi suite.*

Jace pocketed his phone and let out a loud sigh. He turned and glanced at the sleeping space behind him. Clint already had the sleeping alcove in the gooseneck trailer they were pulling and deserved it more than Jace. At least by staying next to the arena, Jace wouldn't have to bother hitching rides back and forth to the motel. He glanced at Clint. "Looks like I'll be sleeping in the cab starting tomorrow night."

4

"You're being sent to a rodeo and getting paid for it? I went into the wrong kind of law, if that's the type of assignment you're getting."

Sydney stared across the lunch table at Erin Kramer, her best friend since law school. They'd chosen an alfresco restaurant on the Chicago River to enjoy the late summer day. "It has nothing to do with my job."

Erin brushed a strand of her strawberry-blond hair out of her eyes. "Your boss assigned you, didn't he?"

"It's a favor, not an actual assignment. I don't know why you find a rodeo so exciting."

Erin selected a chicken taco from the large platter in the center of the table. "I've loved rodeo ever since I was a kid. While I was growing up in Colorado, if there wasn't a rodeo happening on weekends, you'd find me on my horse, riding the trails."

"You've never told me that."

"It's how I got the freckles on my nose. Too much time riding without a hat. It was always blowing off. Since coming to Chicago for college and law school, my life has done a one-eighty, and my rodeo days seem like they happened in the Dark Ages. So what's the reason for this rodeo trip if isn't work-related?"

Sydney helped herself to one of the tacos and set it on her plate. The aroma of chicken and spices wafted to her nose. "I have to convince my boss's nephew to not bail on his sponsor without negotiating a contract cancellation. If he quits cold, he'll pay hefty fines, which he can't afford. I met Jace when he was here two years ago, and Harry thinks that because we already kind of know each other, he'll listen to me."

Sydney looked off at the river and removed her sunglasses as one of the architectural tour boats floated past. Its passengers craned their necks to look up at the skyscraper behind where the women sat, as the tour guide gave a description. She and Jace had sat in a similar boat. In all the years she'd lived in Chicago, she'd never taken the tour, but Jace wanted to go and he'd loved it. She had to admit that since the tour, she'd never looked at the city's buildings the same way.

"Who's the cowboy? I may recognize him by name."

Erin's question broke into Sydney's thoughts. She should have known her friend would want more details than she was willing to give. She replaced her sunglasses and faced Erin. "Jace McGowan. You've probably never heard—"

Erin's eyes rounded to the size of quarters. "Last year's third-place winner in bull riding at the NFR?"

Syd couldn't help but smile at Erin's exuberance. "I thought you said you weren't interested in rodeo anymore. He mentioned wanting to win first place at a competition in Vegas. That's all I know."

"That's the National Rodeo Finals. They're on TV at odd hours, so I usually record them. So you and Jace already talked on the phone?"

"We had lunch at Malnati's yesterday."

Erin raised her palm but didn't seem to notice Sydney's halfhearted palm slap. "I can't believe it. Girl, you're just now telling me this? What's he like? Most rodeo cowboys I've met are really nice and laid-back."

Sydney laughed. "I didn't have lunch with the latest Hollywood heartthrob."

"Don't kid yourself. Jace McGowan is one hot cowboy."

"He's definitely good-looking, but so are a lot of men right here in Chicago, including your own fiancé."

Erin gave a dismissive wave. "No worries. Karl is my one and only, and I love him to pieces. But I still enjoy looking at handsome cowboys too. What happened when he was here two years ago?"

She'd intended to use Erin as a sounding board, but with her friend acting like a starstruck rodeo groupie, maybe it wasn't her best option. She needed someone with less bias to help her sort her thoughts, and time was short. She was leaving tomorrow.

Sydney sipped her iced tea. "He's nice enough. Harry had court and asked me to show him around. We did the tourist thing. Navy Pier, Millennium Park, the architectural tour that just passed by... He wanted to see Wrigley Field, but the Cubs were on the road and we couldn't get in."

Erin shook her head. "Packed day you two had, and you never told me about it."

Sydney stared at the half-eaten taco on her plate. She'd never told anyone about the day or the way Jace had affected her so deeply. By keeping the memory to herself, the day seemed more an aberration than reality. The theory had worked well ... until now. "It was only a day. He was on the road to a rodeo in Cheyenne the next morning."

Erin stared at her as if she'd grown an extra head. "Did he act at all interested?"

Images of their dinner at the top of the Hancock Building flowed into her mind like a slow movie crawl—the city lights below twinkling like tiny diamonds as they came on in the gathering dusk, the best lobster she'd ever tasted, and the kiss when she left him at the curb in front of Harry's home in Wilmette. Her head was spinning so much, she was almost afraid to drive home.

"I can tell by the look on your face that the answer is positive."

Sydney blinked and shook her head, more to dislodge the memory than to deny Erin's statement. "I knew better than to take him seriously. He likely has a broken heart in every town he's competed in."

Erin's smile faded. "I've heard rumors. Never take half that stuff seriously. How do you know about his reputation?"

"Harry warned me before I spent the day with him ... but Jace is different now. He says he's found God and his past is behind him. As for not mentioning him, you were on your trip to Italy when it happened. By the time you arrived home, I was over Jace. And still am. We've got nothing in common."

Erin held up a hand. "Stop. What do you mean, you have nothing in common? Didn't you just say he's a Christian now? That is huge for you, Syd. I've heard you say it many times: if you ever marry, it will have to be to a man of faith."

Sydney forced herself not to wince. "The key word in my statement is *if*. There are other factors to consider. His life is on a ranch in Texas. I'm a city girl and my life is here." She waved her hand in a wide sweep, taking in the river and surrounding high-rises. "Chicago is my home. Besides, I need to be here for Dad's legal clinic."

Erin rolled her eyes. "For what? The clinic has a board and a director in place."

"I owe it to Dad's memory to stay close and volunteer there once I have more time."

"There's more, girlfriend. Your eyes have a faraway look. Spill it."

A dull ache filled Sydney's chest. She'd done so well until yesterday. Erin would never understand if she knew that despite the old feelings returning and Jace being a changed man, Sydney couldn't begin to think about seriously dating him or any other man. For Erin, love trumped all. Karl had moved to Chicago from Germany for her—no chance of him bailing. "There aren't many details to spill."

Erin pushed the taco platter to the side and reached for Sydney's hand and squeezed it. "So what's the problem?"

"Why start something that can't be carried through?" Erin's face blurred, and Sydney pulled her hand from the woman's grasp and dug in her purse for a tissue. Not finding one, she dabbed at her eyes with her napkin. Black smudges of mascara marred the white fabric.

"Long-distance relationships have led to permanent ones before. Karl and

I are prime examples. True love has caused many to move to places they never thought they'd like, and they end up loving it because they're with the one they love."

Sydney heaved a sigh. "Ever the romantic, aren't you?" She dropped the crumpled napkin onto the table and sat up straight. "It's more complicated than distance. I really need to stay here."

"Why can't you fulfill your dad's mission there as well as here?"

"Victory Legal Assistance is here. That's why."

"Again I ask, why does VLA need you here to keep running?"

Sydney shrugged. Erin would never understand. "VLA is my dad's baby, and I'm the only one left who can carry the torch. Once I make partner, I'll be able to divide my time better. And as far as this rodeo trip is concerned, I expect to be back by Saturday afternoon or, at the worst, no later than Sunday."

"What kind of clothes are you planning to take?"

Sydney shrugged. "I suppose work clothes and a pair of jeans."

"Work clothes? Like what you're wearing now?"

Sydney glanced down at her black skirt and teal silk blouse. Her matching suit jacket hung on the back of her chair. "I'll be there to work. My clothes will be appropriate."

Erin laughed and shook her head. "No. Not at a rodeo."

"Who said I'm attending a rodeo? We'll meet at a restaurant or coffee shop near my hotel. No rodeo for me. You know I'm not into horseback riding."

"You won't be riding horses, only watching others ride them. I need to go back to work, but come to my place at 5:30 and I'll loan you all you need so you won't look like the newbie that you are."

Sydney opened her mouth to protest, but Erin held up her a hand, palm out. "Stop. No refusals. Trust me, you don't want to go down there in your business suit."

Jace's phone rang as he carried Charley's feedbag to the horse's pen. He pulled the iPhone from his pocket, glanced at the screen, and was tempted to not answer. Almost every time his mother called, it was more bad news about the tax situation. But he swiped the screen with his thumb anyway. "Hi, Mom. Can I call you back in a sec? I'm just fixin' to feed Charley. We only got to the rodeo grounds a half hour ago, and everyone's hungry."

"I'll wait."

A minute later, Jace strode away from the pen toward the vacant arena and sat on the steps leading up to the VIP viewing platform. "Okay, Charley's a happy horse. What's going on?"

"Another letter from the IRS arrived today. They're requesting a meeting to discuss a payment schedule. I thought Rick Taggart was having the correspondence sent directly to him."

Jace's stomach burned hot, and he bit back a curse word that had been part of his normal vocabulary until last year. *Stay calm. Don't show her you're worried.* "I thought so too. I'll give Taggart a call. Maybe they sent the letter to the attorney's office and just copied us."

"Honey, I'm sorry your dad put you through this."

She sniffed, and Jace imagined her blinking away the tears, which usually came at this point of the conversation. He hated the stress that the back taxes were taking on her. None of it was her fault. Dad had kept the perilous situation hidden from her along with his gambling addiction, which caused the taxes to go into arrears. He knew from the attorney that his father hadn't intentionally left the books in such disarray—he'd been working to pay them off—but the cancer took him before he could clean things up. "That's okay, Mom. It is what it is."

She cleared her throat. "I know, it's just..." She paused and sighed. "How was your visit with Harry?"

"Okay. He arranged for a lawyer to have lunch with me since he was busy. She did her best to talk me into renegotiating with Frisky's."

"She?"

"Yeah, the daughter of Harry's partner who died back when the firm was a two-man operation."

"Jim Knight's daughter works for Harry?"

"Yep. Sydney followed in her daddy's footsteps."

"Sydney. That's her name. I was thinking it was an *S* name, but I wanted to call her *Sybil*. Maybe Harry thought a pretty young woman's persuasive powers would work better than his crusty manner."

"How'd you know she's pretty?"

"I remember Sydney as a pretty little girl and presume she still is. Did it work?"

"You remember her?"

"Sure do. Several times when we visited Jim, his family also came over. You and Corey played with both of their children. The twins weren't born yet. I guess you were too young to remember."

He, Corey, and Syd were childhood playmates? He'd rarely played with girls when he was a boy. Had he treated her nicely or beat up on her?

"Did she persuade you to renegotiate?"

He should tell Mom that he intended to renegotiate, to put her mind at ease, but he'd decided to stall Syd as long as possible over the weekend to give them more time to reconnect. He couldn't risk Mom telling his uncle and then Uncle Harry telling Syd before the end of the weekend. "The pizza was great."

"Are you seeing her again?"

"Why?"

"To talk more about the contract."

"Harry's sending her down here tomorrow to discuss it. Don't worry. What she said at lunch made some sense, but I still have some questions before I decide what to do." He drew in a deep breath and let it out slowly. If she only knew how many nights he'd lain awake. He'd always found it easy to compartmentalize his problems and "cowboy up" with a smile on his face, knowing that if he gave in to fretting and worrying, he'd be no good to the ranch work or to the bull riding. But never had the stakes been as high as now. It was taking a toll on him.

"Mom, I'm not going to let anything happen to cause us to lose the ranch. I'd never forgive myself if I did. I'll call the tax attorney right away and let you know if you should fax it over to him."

After they said their good-byes, he disconnected and stared at the phone. Why wouldn't he have remembered playing with Sydney and her brother when they were kids? Then he chuckled. Like his young niece Amanda, Syd probably always insisted on wearing a frilly dress. He'd once tried to get Amanda on a ranch pony, and she was so scared that she'd had a meltdown.

Jace refocused and went to his contact list on the phone. He tapped on his lawyer's name. He not only needed to let Taggart know about the letter from the IRS but also to find out whether he'd gotten his message to start negotiations with Frisky's and to hold off mentioning it to his mom.

Sydney entered the lobby of Erin's apartment building and pressed the buzzer next to her friend's name. When the security door buzzed, she let herself in and headed for the elevator. Arriving at the fifth floor, she turned left. Erin stood in the hallway several doors down, grinning and wearing a cowboy hat, with her hair in braids that fell over her shoulders.

Sydney laughed. "You look like you just finished roping a calf. I really think I should tell Harry to have *you* talk to Jace. Come to think of it, if you weren't engaged, you'd be a good match for him."

Erin took her by the arm and pulled her inside the apartment. "And happily engaged, I may add. I'm afraid I may have given you the wrong idea with all my cowboy talk this afternoon." Her diamond ring flashed in the entry hall's overhead light.

Sydney drew Erin into a hug. "No wrong idea on my part. I knew you were saying those things for my benefit. Karl is the perfect match for you." She moved farther into the apartment toward the overstuffed couch.

"Not there. We have business in the guest room." Erin pointed to the hall that led to the bedrooms. "Come with me."

Sydney stepped into the room Erin had decorated to resemble a spa-like retreat. Across the bed lay two pairs of jeans and a couple of Western-style long-sleeved shirts. A pair of polished brown boots sat on the floor beside the bed. She faced her friend. "Where did you get all this?"

"In my closet. I lived in those clothes when I was in Colorado. We're about the same size. The boots should fit if you wear them with thick socks. I insist you take them." She took off the cowboy hat and plopped it onto Sydney's head. "Hey, it looks cute on you."

Sydney removed the hat and tossed it onto the bed. She tugged on one of Erin's braids. "Silly girl. I'm only planning to be there for a day."

"I thought you said you may come back on Sunday. I looked on the rodeo's website. That means four nights and at least two rodeos—Friday night and Saturday night. You need to be prepared. Now, if you stay till Monday, there is a rodeo Sunday ni—"

"Stop." Sydney walked to the window and stared out at the brick wall belonging to the apartment building next door. She hadn't even thought to research the rodeo. "I repeat, I have no intention of attending even one rodeo. I'm hoping we can discuss the contract over dinner tomorrow night, he'll agree to renegotiate, and I'll even be home by Thursday."

"What if he doesn't agree that fast?"

"He will." She touched the horseshoe pendant hanging from the chain on her neck. Jace had to agree by tomorrow night. She had only enough in her to keep her guard up for that long.

"Humor me."

Sydney turned. "Right now, I feel quite humorless."

Erin picked up a pale-blue plaid shirt and unbuttoned it. "Try this on to make sure—with the jeans."

"I have jeans."

"Skinny jeans, yes. And they look great on you. But you need a boot-cut pair."

"I'll tuck the jeans into the boots."

"Not how it's done at rodeos."

Sydney rolled her eyes. "I'm not attending any rodeo, remember?"

Erin averted her gaze and let out a heavy sigh as her shoulders slumped.

Sydney took in a ragged breath and stared at her feet. Erin had gone to so much trouble to help her not look like a misfit, and here Sydney was, thinking only of herself. It wouldn't hurt to accept Erin's offer. She could take the clothes and leave them in the suitcase. "Let's see how this blouse fits. I love the color." Sydney slipped off her blouse and stuck her arms into the sleeves of Erin's shirt.

"Where'd you get that necklace? It's beautiful."

Sydney continued buttoning the shirt, relieved that Erin's spirits had lifted. "It was a gift from my dad. All this talk about horses and rodeos reminded me of it. I dug it out of my jewelry box on a whim before I came over."

"I thought you weren't interested in horses."

"My dad was always trying to get me to like them." She grabbed the pair of dark blue jeans and put them on.

"A perfect fit. Sit on the bed, and I'll help you get the boots on." Erin knelt on the floor in front of Sydney, then pulled gym socks out of the boots and slipped them over Sydney's bare feet.

A moment later, Sydney stood. She'd forgotten how good boots always felt when she rode with Dad. "Everything fits just fine." She stepped over to a full-length mirror attached to the closet door. One look at her reflection made more memories flood over her.

Dad had given her a similar outfit for her twelfth birthday along with the horseshoe pendant. He'd stood behind her as she faced a mirror. "There's my girl," he'd said. "So grown up and ready for her own horse." Sydney spun around and hugged him. "My own horse?"

He'd grinned back at her. "Come get in the car. We're heading out to the stables."

She'd ridden Honey as much as possible until that fateful day four years later. After that, she never rode again and Honey was sold a year later.

"By the expression on your face—if I didn't know better—I'd think you were heading off for a few days of misery."

Sydney started and faced Erin. She forced a smile. "Nothing to do with the clothes. Thanks for the loan."

5

Sydney parked her Prius in a space next to the Prairieland Hotel in Robinson, Illinois. As much as she'd tried to think about something else during the almost-five-and-a-half-hour drive, Jace had stayed in the forefront of her mind. The guy was drop-dead gorgeous, but more than that, what she'd seen of the man he'd become made him even more attractive than the first time she fell for him. And that scared her. She had to think of Jace as a client; otherwise she'd find herself in so deep emotionally, she'd never find a path to safety.

She gathered her purse from the passenger seat and opened the car door. Hot air rushed into the vehicle. Her car thermometer hadn't budged from the 99-degree mark since she'd left the interstate an hour and a half ago. The room Jace reserved for her might not be more than a single bed and bathroom, but if it had a working air conditioner, she'd be fine.

Sydney surveyed the almost-empty parking lot and the well-kept grounds. If the inside of the hotel was as presentable as the outside, she could dismiss her fears of run-down accommodations. There was no sign of Jace, but then, they hadn't agreed to meet here. She mentally shook her head at herself. She shouldn't have expected him to meet her. This was a business trip, not a weekend getaway with a boyfriend. She walked to the car's rear and opened the hatch. After lifting her suitcase to the ground, she telescoped the handle to a workable height and rolled it toward the hotel entrance.

With a head of bouncing curls and a smile that never left her face, a cheerful desk clerk greeted her. Within minutes, Sydney was checked in. "You have the best accommodation in the house," the clerk declared. "The cowboys like the room a lot."

Sydney took the key-card packet the clerk held out. "Why is that?"

"You'll see. You're lucky to get it. The suite was booked through the weekend, but it became available late yesterday."

Sydney's mouth dropped open. "Suite?"

The woman's eyes twinkled. "Not as fancy as what those big-city hotels have, but it's quite nice."

Sydney thanked her, grabbed her suitcase by the handle, and headed for the elevator. All she'd needed was a good air conditioner, but as long as Harry was paying, she'd enjoy the suite. Although, the clerk had said it suddenly became free late yesterday ... which was about the same time Harry was talking to Jace on the phone. Sydney frowned. It was one thing for Jace to pull some strings, but if he'd wheeled and dealed someone right out of their reservation, they'd have to have a talk.

She stepped off the elevator and almost ran into a large cart piled high with clean towels and linens. She smiled at the young dark-haired woman wearing a uniform with the hotel logo and maneuvered her suitcase around the obstruction.

Sydney stopped in front of the room indicated on the key-card envelope and slid the magnetic card into the slot. A few steps inside the suite, she relaxed. It was more an oversized typical hotel room than a suite. She could live with this. Especially the large claw-foot tub in the sleeping alcove.

She kicked off her sandals and padded into the alcove. The tub may have looked old-fashioned, but it wasn't her grandmother's claw-foot. Not with jets that shot pulsating water. She picked up one of the bottles of bath gel from a decorative wire basket straddling the width of the tub, removed the top, and sniffed. Jasmine—one of her favorites. But definitely not a masculine scent. So why was this room a favorite of the cowboys? Of course, who wouldn't want a soak in a Jacuzzi tub after a night of bucking bulls? She checked her watch. If she hurried, she could try out the tub before Jace called. She got hot water flowing into the tub, then grabbed her suitcase and lifted it onto the bed.

The room phone rang, and she walked to where it sat on the bedside table and answered it.

"Syd, are you here?" Her stomach dipped. *Easy, girl. Remember, he's only a client.*

She drew in a breath. *Focus, Sydney, focus.*

"Syd?"

"Hi, Jace." She cleared her throat. "I arrived about a half hour ago."

"Do you like the room?"

He sounded like a kid who'd just spent his entire allowance on a present for her. "It's lovely, but—"

"Good to hear. When do you want to get together?"

"Can we meet tonight? If we settle this misunderstanding with your contract, I can head back to Chicago tomorrow and be out of your way."

"You're never in my way, Syd. And I don't misunderstand my contract at all. I just don't want to play with Frisky's anymore."

Maybe he should tell that to Frisky's himself instead of letting an attorney do it for him. With that Texas drawl, he'll have them eating out of his hand in no time. "By the way, the desk clerk mentioned that some people had the room booked through the weekend but then they suddenly canceled. I hope you didn't throw your weight around. A smaller room would have been adequate."

"You don't like a jetted tub? I thought you'd be pleased with that."

"Yes, of course I do, but—"

"I thought you'd appreciate having a sofa to stretch out on while you worked, rather than sitting in a straight chair."

She glanced at the cozy arrangement of an overstuffed couch and two matching chairs on the opposite side of the room. "I'm sure a sofa is more comfortable, but I don't expect to be here long enough to use it. About the pressure you must have—"

"I don't have *that* much weight to throw around. I must have asked at the right time. Maybe it was a God thing."

Sydney frowned. "Do you think He cares what kind of room I have?"

"Remember, He knows every hair on our heads."

He had her there, but did that include hotel accommodations? Out of the mouths of newbie Christians. "And so He does. Now, about our meeting ... is there a coffee shop where we can meet this evening?"

"Possibly around Robinson, but I don't have wheels unless I drive the front end of the rig, which is pretty much set up to stay where it's at since it's attached to the trailer. Can you come to the arena? We'll find someplace to talk around here."

Dad had only hauled a two-horse trailer behind his truck, not one of those fancier ones that included living quarters the way Jace had described, but she'd seen cabs on the road without a trailer attached. So what stopped them from detaching the trailer? "It sounds complicated to release the cab."

"Well, it's not as easy as it may look. We prefer to leave the setup intact."

She didn't have many options, then. She wouldn't have to leave the car. She'd pick him up and they'd drive to a convenient place to talk. "Okay. I'll come your way and we'll find a Starbucks or something. I was thinking maybe in a couple of hours?"

His deep chuckle came through the connection. "We're in the middle of corn and soybean fields. You'll have to settle for 'or something' since there's no Starbucks around here. We'll have to meet soon, though, as I may have something going on later."

A vision of Jace spending the evening with a cute barrel racer materialized. An ache filled her chest at thoughts of what might have been, had they not gone their separate ways two years ago. She gave herself a mental readjustment. *Enough already.*

"Syd? Is earlier okay?"

She checked the time on the bedside clock. "Yes. I'll change and be there in however long it takes to get to you. You do have my cell phone number, don't you?"

"Yeah. Uncle Harry gave it to me. But the cell service is bad down here unless you are on the only carrier that serves this area. If you don't have it, it's spotty."

"And you have the right service, I presume. Which one is that?"

He named the service and asked which one she had. "Unfortunately, not that one."

"Hey, you're not totally cut off. Other services do work on occasion."

All the more reason to wrap up this trip quickly. "Tell me how to get to the arena." She jotted down the directions, and after they disconnected, she let the water out of the tub. A good soak before bed was better anyway. With an agreement from Jace to renegotiate the contract, she'd be ready to wash him out of her life for good.

Robinson's business district, complete with a courthouse square, could have passed for the town in *It's a Wonderful Life*. Jace might have been right about the town of Palestine not having a coffee shop, but apparently Robinson didn't have one either. Nor a diner on the main drag. Where did the locals meet to discuss business or even the latest town gossip?

A sign displaying a picture of a large coffee cup came into view. *Yes!* When Sydney got closer, her spirits crashed. The Java Hut was no larger than a child's playhouse ... but at least the drive-up window assured her of getting a vanilla latte in the morning.

Railroad tracks parallel to the highway kept her company for several miles as she passed browning cornstalks and a few farmhouses. Suddenly the road made a sharp turn right, crossed the tracks, and made another sharp turn left. She'd arrived in "Historic Palestine, Illinois"—or at least that's what the sign in between the two turns had said.

Following Jace's instructions, Sydney drove down a leafy street lined with small bungalows, turned, and a block later turned again. She emerged into an open area. A cemetery on her right assured her that she wasn't lost. Ahead, a sign spelled out Pioneer City Arena in large letters. She'd come to the right place. Her pulse raced as she sped up. Her traitorous heart hadn't gotten the message that the man was off-limits.

Sydney rolled up to a stop sign across from the arena entrance, her focus still on the sign. *Now what? He never said where to meet him.* Then she dropped her gaze and her stomach fluttered. All questions answered.

The man should be arrested for being so good-looking.

Jace stepped away from the fence post he'd been using as a prop and waved as he sauntered across the road. His long-sleeved shirt—a blue plaid this time—gave a hint of the man's muscular body beneath. As he strode closer, he radiated confidence like a badge of honor.

His blue-eyed gaze peered from beneath the brim of his black Stetson and locked with hers. She lowered her window without breaking the connection. He leaned his forearms on the window ledge and brought his head to eye level. The intoxicating scent of his woodsy cologne wafted over to her. "Welcome to my world, Sydney Knight."

Her stomach flipped, and she dropped her gaze to his darkened jaw and the full lips it framed. Lips that had sent her heart soaring into the ether more than two years earlier, though it seemed like yesterday. "Thank you."

He straightened. "Unlock the passenger door so I can hop in and direct you to my home away from home."

No. He was doing it all wrong. No meeting on his turf allowed. "Can't we go somewhere to talk directly from here?"

"I want to show you something first. Humor me?"

She opened her mouth to say that she wasn't dressed for walking on grass or dirt but then closed it. Best to keep quiet. If she stayed in the car, she'd be okay. She released the locks as Jace rounded the vehicle's rear and opened the front passenger door. Warm humid air came with him as he slid onto the seat.

He slammed the door and flashed her a crooked grin, deepening his dimples. "The air-conditioning feels mighty good." He removed his hat and held it on his lap.

"I thought you Texans liked the heat."

"I've learned to tolerate it, but it doesn't mean I like it much." He ran his gaze over her and his eyes widened. "That's a mighty fine suit you're wearing, but I thought you'd at least wear jeans. This is the rodeo, Sydney. You're not in Chicago anymore."

Her cheeks warmed. Good thing Erin wasn't there, or she'd be hearing "I told you so" for the next hour at least. She cast about for a good comeback but was left wanting. "We're to have a business meeting, not attend a rodeo." She wanted a do-over.

He rolled his eyes. "I'm sure Uncle Harry didn't mean you had to dress for the office down here. I guarantee he wouldn't have shown up in one of his designer suits. Go through the gate over there and hang a right, and then do a quick left."

He was dead-on about Harry. Hopefully Jace wouldn't tell his uncle about this, or she'd never hear the end of it, same as with Erin. Best to keep calm and carry on, as the saying went. At the *click* of Jace's seat belt, she pressed her foot on the gas. The car didn't move. She tried again, but the car didn't respond.

Great. What a time for the car to break down. "It was fine a minute ago."

Jace leaned over the gearshift, and his deep chuckle filled the car. "It might help if you put it in Drive."

She jerked the gearshift into the correct position and hit the accelerator. The car shot across the road and through the open gate.

Jace gripped the door handle.

She slammed her foot onto the brakes and the car skidded to a stop inches from a fence. "And for my next trick..."

He let out a whoosh of air. "Ridin' a bull is safer than ridin' with you."

Heat filled her face, and this time it wasn't because of his masculine charm. He must think her a ditz. "Sorry if I scared you."

"Surprised is more like it—scared, not so much." The right corner of his lip hiked up. "Shall we try again?"

Soothed by his lack of mockery, she gingerly pressed her foot on the gas and made the turns as he directed. They rolled down a paved lane that cut between two large grassy areas. Ahead on the right, metal bleachers came into view. "Should I stop?"

"Keep going. The rig is beyond all this." A moment later, Jace gestured with his thumb to a high wooden fence off to their right that blocked their view. "The arena is on the other side. One of the best I've seen. The townspeople actually built it themselves."

The lane ended and he directed her across the grass to a long white trailer attached to the kind of truck cab usually connected with a semi, just like he'd described. She parked a few feet away from what Jace referred to as "the rig."

"My boys are over in the pens." Jace pointed toward a maze of corrals made from silver piping. "I've got four bulls with me this trip."

Sydney gazed at the trailer. It was longer than most horse trailers she'd seen but similar. "All the bulls fit in there?"

"Yep. And Charley too."

"Who's Charley?"

"My horse. I'm entered in the calf roping on Saturday night."

Her pulse ramped up. She hadn't been near a horse since her dad died, and she had no desire to be near one now. He wouldn't dare ask her to walk over to see his animals. Not with her wearing office clothes and stilettos—

Jace opened his door. "Let's get a closer look." He climbed out and slammed the door behind him.

Sydney stiffened. *Seriously?* She caught a glimpse of him in her rearview mirror as he rounded the Prius.

Jace flung open her door and Sydney stared at his outstretched hand. What a time to find out that chivalry wasn't dead after all. Maybe she could fake a sudden headache. No, bad idea. Lying was never good. Those animals were his pride and joy, his livelihood. To refuse would hurt his feelings.

Sydney released her seat belt, then turned and placed her feet on the grass. *If he knew how much I paid for these Bruno Magli's, he'd probably choke.* She scanned the grass between her car and the pen—lush, green, and devoid of any foreign objects better known as cow patties, she hoped. She pushed to her feet, and all four inches of her stiletto heels sank into the earth.

Sydney tugged at her right foot and teetered first forward and then backward. She flailed her arms. *I'm going down.*

Jace grabbed her elbow and steadied her. "Didn't you bring any other shoes?"

She didn't miss the incredulous tone in his voice, and she couldn't blame him. "Back at the hotel."

Sydney leaned against his arm and pulled against her right foot. The heel popped out. Trying to land on the ball of her foot, she took a step. The heel sank. She may as well have been standing in quicksand. After hauling in a deep breath, she strained at the leg and tipped backward.

Jace's arm went around her waist, and she fell against his hard chest.

Sydney looked up at him and chuckled. "Nice catch, cowboy. Thanks."

"The pleasure is all mine," he drawled. "I'm here to serve."

Silence fell. One beat, then two. Neither moved. Perspiration trickled down her neck. *Awkward.*

Sydney leaned forward, and Jace relaxed his hold but kept his arm positioned behind her. She slipped off her suit jacket and tossed it onto the car seat. "Maybe if I walk on the balls of my feet, I can make it to the fence." She forced a smile. "Then can we find a nearby restaurant where we can talk?"

"You don't have to go to the pens. My fault for expecting you to"—he ran his gaze down her frame—"dressed the way you are. Maybe tomorrow."

But we need to wrap this up tonight. "I'll be okay. Let's go."

He winked. "Your wish is my command. Put your hand on my shoulder and I'll help you free your shoes. We'll walk slowly."

Sydney pulled at her right leg, and the heel popped out. She kicked off the shoe and set her bare foot on the ground. The cool grass felt wonderful against her skin. She did the same with the other foot and dropped the shoe next to its mate. "If I were sure I wouldn't step on something I shouldn't, I'd go barefoot."

Jace's face brightened. "Wait in the car for a minute. I'll be right back." He jogged toward the trailer.

Sydney took a step backward and dropped into the car seat. Was he going to bring her his boots? Her size eights would swim in anything he wore. She fished in her purse for an elastic band and caught up her hair into a ponytail. Not her usual business look, but the long hair was beginning to make her feel as if she were wearing a winter scarf.

The trailer door swung open and Jace held up a pair of brown cowboy boots. "These should fit," he said as he strode across the grass. "They belong to my cousin Lacy."

He handed her a boot. She ran her fingertips over the stitched leather, then peeked inside one of them and spotted what she was looking for. "They're only a half size larger than mine." Jace handed her a sock next. She put it on, then set the boot on the ground and slipped her foot inside. She got the other boot on as well and then tossed the red heels onto the floor of her backseat without checking the damage. If she did, she'd probably cry.

Jace watched with an expectant expression on his face as she stood. "Feel okay?"

Sydney nodded. "Not exactly what a well-dressed lawyer wears to work, but they'll do. Good job, cowboy. Now, let's see those bulls."

"Where I come from, people wear boots all the time. Even with office clothes." His gaze ran her length. "The boots look good on you. You may as well keep them until you leave."

His approval warmed her, but she worked to keep her facial expression stoic. The last thing she wanted was for him to see her pleasure. "Won't Lacy need her boots when she arrives?"

"Nah. They've been in the trailer since spring. She's probably forgotten all about them."

"I meant what I said, Jace. I plan to leave as soon as you agree to negotiate a cancellation, and I expect that to happen tonight."

"You think I'm going to cave that quickly? I hope you at least brought some jeans for Friday night's rodeo."

Sydney stared up at the sky, then back at him. If he expected her to stay for forty-eight hours, he was wrong. She had to leave sooner than that. Her sanity depended on it.

They neared the bulls, and a beautiful black-and-white horse in the next pen stepped out from the shadows.

"That's Charley. We can go over and say hello before we leave."

Sydney glanced off to their right. "You said the townspeople built this arena? I'd like to see it before we go."

Jace gave her a blank stare. "Um. Sure. But I've been ignoring Charley most of the day, and he needs some attention. It won't take long. He doesn't realize that, after our meeting, I'm going to give him a workout over there." He pointed to a large green pasture off to their left.

She brought her eyes back to his paint quarter horse and heaviness filled her chest. She pushed the sensation of regret away. She'd made her choice years ago, and what was done was done.

"Sydney. You okay?

She lifted her chin. "I'm fine. Take me to the bulls."

6

Grateful for the boots, Sydney followed Jace to the fence rail. Four huge bulls—two brown, one black, and one black and white, all with horns that could pass for lethal weapons—stood unmoving, munching on grass. The black-and-white one gave them a disinterested glance and wandered to the pen's far side. He lowered himself to his knees and then to the ground and curled in his front feet. His lids lowered as his muscular body relaxed. Even with his girth and horns, the brute gave the impression that a person could walk up and pet him.

In the next pen, Charley hadn't stood still since they'd walked up to the rails ... much the way Sydney's horse, Honey, had acted when she first saw Sydney after an absence. A dull ache returned to her chest and she directed her attention to the bulls to think about something else. "I'm surprised they're so docile."

"Most times they are, until they get in the chute and the gate opens. Then they know it's time to go to work." Jace flashed a smile. "Look at Charley over there. Want to meet him?"

Yes, in the worst way. "No, thanks. I'll wait here."

"He won't bite."

"I know. But I'd rather not."

His lips parted as though he were about to say something. Instead, he shrugged and sauntered toward the black-and-white horse. "Hey, boy, I know you're itching for a run. We'll get one in after I meet with Sydney."

The horse nuzzled his chest. Jace laughed and pulled something from his shirt pocket. He held out his open hand. "Can't keep any secrets from you, can I?" While the horse gobbled the treats, Jace looked over his shoulder at Sydney and grinned. "See? Gentle as can be."

She managed a smile and turned away. Why couldn't she have given it over to God and gone to the horse? Because if she did, she'd likely forget that she wasn't supposed to be interested in horses and start rubbing his head and talking to him in the way Honey had liked. The more Jace didn't know how much they had in common, the less he'd ask many questions.

Jace sauntered to her side. "What is it you hold against horses?"

Like that question. Sydney swatted at a bug flying around her face. "I don't have anything against them. I prefer my pets small and furry."

He rested his right foot on the lower fence rail and leaned his forearms on the top one. "I'll give you the short version on the boys." He pointed to the black-and-white bull. "That's Oreo, my newest bull. His daddy is Ugly Man, the rankest bull in the PBR pen until he retired a couple of years ago. I expect great things from Oreo."

"PBR? Someone mentioned something else with different initials. The NBR? They remembered your name as coming in third. Is it the same thing?"

He smiled. "You know someone who follows rodeo?"

Sydney shrugged. "A friend from law school."

"That's cool. NFR, where I placed third last year, is the National Finals Rodeo. The most-winning people in the PRCA go there to compete. The rodeo right here is a PRCA-sanctioned rodeo."

She rolled her eyes. "You're confusing me with all these acronyms. But I guess some of ours in the legal world would sound like alphabet soup to you."

"You got that right. I've already heard a mess of them from my attorneys. PRCA stands for Professional Rodeo Cowboy Association. Professional Bull Riders—PBR for short—is an organization made up only of bull riders. It's the big kahuna. I'm hoping to make the cut to buck in their events by next year. A win at their finals means a cool mill in the pocket."

She felt her eyes round. "That much money? Has rodeo always been so lucrative?"

"If you make it to the NFR, it can be. Place in the PBR in their top-tier events, and you can make a decent living throughout the season, not just at finals. PBR riders have an easier time with getting good sponsors and endorsements, which helps too."

"As long as the sponsors meet your criteria." She frowned and tilted her head. "Sorry for so many questions. You said Oreo's father was the rankest bull. What does *rank* mean?"

He grinned. "I'm loving your questions. *Rank* in bull jargon means 'tough to ride.' So far, Oreo's unridden—meaning he's bucked off every cowboy who's drawn him."

"Don't you want the cowboys to ride?"

"As a stock contractor, I want my bulls to buck off the riders. When that happens, they get higher points and I get more money." He pushed his hat back on his head and faced her directly. "As a bull rider, I want to stay on any bull I ride for eight seconds and not wreck. Then I'll have a chance at the purse—the word for winnings."

She frowned. "Wreck as in have an accident?"

"Yeah. A bad accident, as in injuries that keep you from bucking for a long time."

A vision of Jace hitting the ground headfirst filled her thoughts. She forced it away. "Only eight seconds?"

"When you're on a rank bull's back, eight seconds can feel like a lifetime."

"So you stay on and then you win something."

"I wish it were that easy. Each ride is scored, half for the cowboy and half for the bull. The ranker the bull, the higher his score. The cowboy is judged on his ability to stay on center, how much spurring he does, and other things. Only those who place win money. Sometimes, in the larger events, it can even go to fifth place."

Sydney frowned. "I hope you guys use blunted spurs." She clamped her mouth shut.

Jace's eyes widened. "How do you know about spurs?"

"I don't know. Maybe something I read somewhere." Her chest tightened. Not exactly a fib, but it sure wasn't the truth.

"I'll give Charley the rest of his treat and we can leave." Jace pulled a couple of brown nuggets from a jeans pocket.

She glanced at his hand. "Equestreats. I used to..." She snapped her mouth shut again and turned toward the Prius. If she dug the hole any deeper, she'd fall into it. "I'll start for the car and meet you there."

Jace lightly gripped her arm. "Wait a minute. First the spurs and now Equestreats... What gives, Syd? I thought you didn't like horses."

She let out a loud sigh. She couldn't lie again. "I used to ride some, but I haven't in years. The idea of getting on a horse now scares me." She tugged her arm out of his grasp and started toward the car.

Sydney arrived at the car and glanced over her shoulder. Jace remained at the pen, arms resting on the top rail and staring straight ahead. Whatever he was thinking, at least he knew not to expect her to come back here again.

She sat on the edge of the driver's seat and wiped the mud and grass from her high heels with the paper towels she had in the car before putting them on her feet. When she got the car started and the A/C blowing, Jace turned from the fence rail and strode across the grass. She'd given him her undivided attention; now it was time for him to return the favor.

Jace opened the passenger door and slid onto the seat, removing his Stetson. He tossed it onto the backseat and faced the front. The chilled air hit his face. "The A/C sure feels good." He glanced at her feet. "I see you have your work shoes back on. Not a trace of grass on them."

She put the car in gear without looking at him. "They were pretty dirty. Boots may be your work shoes, but they're not mine." A smile lifted the corners of her mouth. "Unless we're talking fashion boots. Chicago winters can be brutal."

"So I've heard. Maybe you should consider moving to Texas."

She cast a quick glance at him. "What do you mean by that?"

"Not a thing. Texas is a big place."

The car bumped across the grass toward the paved lane. When they reached the road, she braked and faced him. "Where are we headed?"

"Back to Robinson for the best smoked meat this area has to offer."

She glared at him.

He chuckled. "Don't go giving me the old stink-eye. They have fish and chicken there too."

"You are incorrigible." She grabbed the roll of paper towels from the space between the seats and threw it at him. He ducked and it hit the window.

Jace clicked his seat belt closed and settled back on the seat. He hadn't missed the grin on her face before she threw the towels. There was a gal with a sense of humor beneath the facade, and he couldn't wait to draw that lady out into the open for good.

He chose to keep his gaze on the small bungalows they passed until they came to the highway at the edge of town and Sydney sped up. Then he stole a glance at her. Wisps of wavy blond hair had worked their way out of her ponytail and were lifting in the cool breeze coming through the vents. Her face wasn't makeup-free, but she wasn't all painted up either. Did she realize how pretty she was? He fought the urge to reach over and trace his fingers along her jawline.

He was as crazy about her now as he had been two years ago, and he only had a few days to find out what it was that caused her to fear horses. He suspected that had been one of her reasons for calling them "mismatched." Something told him she might be willing to admit feelings for him if he could uncover this secret of hers in time. He had to figure out a way to help her fears. Maybe when Lacy arrived, she could give a hand. The assistance might go over better with a woman. That, and stalling to agree to renegotiate, should keep Syd there at least through Friday night.

Sydney turned into the Back Porch Smokehouse lot and parked. At least Jace had kept silent during the drive and she'd managed to force her liar's guilt into a compartment in the back of her mind. This was a business meeting and nothing more. They'd discuss, he'd agree to renegotiate, and they'd eat. Then, first thing tomorrow, she'd bid the Jacuzzi tub and the cowboy good-bye and head back to Chicago. Her heart squeezed. If only it were as easy as that.

Jace pointed to the movie theater next to the restaurant. "Maybe we can catch a flick after we eat."

She loved movies, but to sit next to him in a darkened theater with his scent of woodsy cologne and horse wafting over to her? No way. She faced him and forced a smile. "After we finish our dinner meeting, I intend to return to the hotel and prepare for my trip home tomorrow."

He threw his head back and laughed. "You're mighty sure of yourself, aren't you?"

"You're a logical man, and I trust you'll see that prolonging this debate any longer is a waste of time. Not to mention the fines you'll receive and how your reputation in the bull-riding community is at stake. Shall we go in?" She opened her door and climbed out. Solid ground had never felt so good.

He grabbed his hat and joined her as she was retrieving her briefcase and purse from the backseat. "What happened to the playful woman who attacked me with a roll of paper towels?"

Sydney liked the paper-towel-tossing woman better too, but she had to keep her playful side on lockdown—for his good as much as hers. She straightened and slipped the carrying straps of her briefcase over her shoulder. "Do you think I'll need my jacket? Is the A/C usually set on freezing in there?"

The twinkle had left his eyes. "You'd better take the jacket."

Sydney grabbed the garment, then slammed the car door shut with her hip.

They reached the rustic building's covered porch. A family sat at one of the tables, with the dad gnawing on a rib bone and the wife eating what looked like fried fish. Their boy had his mouth wrapped around a cheeseburger. Jace held the door open, and Sydney stepped through. The aroma of smoked meat barbeque settled around them, and her stomach rumbled. A young woman wearing Daisy Dukes and a T-shirt scurried toward them, her gaze never leaving Jace as she crossed the dining room. She flashed him a wide smile and batted eyelashes that looked long enough to skateboard on. "Hello, cowboy. Back so soon?"

Jace laughed. "I come here as often as possible when I'm in town. Last night, tonight, and at least one more time, if I have my way."

The girl giggled. "I'm glad you came during my shift again."

Feeling quite invisible, Sydney resisted the urge to slip her arm through

Jace's and say something syrupy-sweet. Not that she had any hold on the man, but for all the girl knew, she could be his wife.

Jace offered a crooked smile. "I am too. Good to see you again."

The girl looked as though she may faint on the spot. "Are you getting ready to compete in the rodeo?" She pushed a lock of nearly black hair behind her left ear and tilted her head. "I'd love to watch you ride."

Sydney waited for Jace to respond. Now was the time for him to prove himself a changed man. Would he be able to resist the come-on?

Jace shoved his hands into his jeans pockets and rocked back on his heels. "I'm sure there are still tickets available. Friday night usually has the lightest attendance—the high school football game competes against us."

The gleam in the girl's eyes dialed down several hundred watts. "I was hoping you'd maybe have some passes."

He shook his head. "Not from me, sorry."

Her half smile melted into a stony expression. "Thanks. I'll check into it."

Jace glanced around the dining room. "Looks like the dinner crowd hasn't arrived yet. We'd like a small table in a quiet corner so we can talk."

The girl turned her gaze to Sydney as though seeing her for the first time. "Oh. Sure thing. Follow me."

Sydney trailed behind the waitress, who no longer walked with a spring in her step. Jace caught up with them as the girl climbed a couple of steps to a dimly lit platform resembling a porch.

"This is the quietest spot we have." The girl indicated a counter-height table tucked into a corner.

After the waitress took their drink orders and left, Jace sat across from Sydney. "Is it my imagination, or did that girl's mood change during the time we walked to this table?"

Sydney looked up from studying the single-page menu. "She was crushing on you and hoping you'd offer her rodeo tickets and a night on the town afterward. She hardly noticed I was with you until you asked for a quiet corner."

"You got all that from a simple conversation?"

"What did you say to her yesterday?"

"We had a friendly discussion about the rodeo, that's all. Nothing to lead her on."

"It doesn't take much for a young girl to get all dreamy-eyed about a good-looking guy who pays attention to her—especially a cowboy. I suppose you gave her a good tip too."

He grinned. "Yeah, come to think of it, I did. You're good, Syd. You wouldn't want to be my manager, would you?"

"Sounds intriguing. But is it wise?"

"You're right. We might stray into where we left off last time."

Sydney hid behind her menu. He'd passed her test with flying colors and wasn't even aware of it. She skimmed the bill of fare. Outside of a couple items, everything on it was beef or pork. It may be called the "other white meat," but pork was usually not her choice.

Jace's hand appeared at the top of the large page and pushed the menu down until they looked eye to eye. "Looks like your selections are limited to catfish or a chicken sandwich. I really thought they had more for you. We can go somewhere else."

Sydney's stomach fluttered. Did he have any idea how mesmerizing his eyes were? She laid her menu on the table. "Thanks, but it's okay. The catfish sounds fine. I'll get the steamed veggies and a baked potato for my sides."

His dimples deepened. "For me, it's between the ribs or the cowboy-cut prime rib. I think I hear the prime rib calling my name."

The waitress returned with their drinks, took their orders, and left. Sydney pulled the contract folder and her iPad from her briefcase. She waited for Jace to stop scrolling through something on his phone. "I hope you're looking for your lawyer's number, because you're going to need it."

He looked up. "Sorry. Just checking e-mail for something from my tax attorney. Not the one you're thinking of." He darkened the phone and set it on the tabletop. "I'm all ears."

"I've typed out some points stating why you need to dissolve the contract, along with what you should be willing to pay them. All subject to your approval. Once we finalize this, you'll have something concrete to take to your attorney— or do you have a manager who deals with your contracts?"

Jace cocked his head. "Can't we talk business after we eat? I'd rather hear more about who Sydney Knight is away from the office."

It didn't take much to see that he was as interested in her as he had been two years earlier. She yearned to throw caution to the wind, but the risk of heading into territory she swore she'd never go to again was too great. She turned on the iPad. "I think we should discuss as much as possible before the food comes. You didn't answer my question about—"

"Daddy, let's sit up there."

Sydney looked toward the main dining area. A small boy wearing a black cowboy hat pulled on his dad's hand. The same waitress stood next to a table a few feet away from them, but the boy continued to pull on his father's hand. The mother, who carried a toddler girl wearing a pink cowboy hat, said something and the dad nodded. The waitress shrugged and led the family up the steps to the raised platform. She gave Sydney a look that appeared apologetic for what was likely to be a noisy family.

Sydney turned her attention to her iPad. "As I started to say, I made up a list of talking points." She tapped on the tablet's screen and her document came to life.

Jace twisted in his seat and grinned at the boy. "How are ya, partner?"

The boy giggled.

An ache filled Sydney's chest. *Likes children and is comfortable with them.* Another box checked. She'd done away with that pointless list a long time ago, so why did it keep resurrecting? "Jace, did you hear me?"

He turned back around. "Sorry. Those kids are cute."

"They're adorable, but we need to get your business discussed before our dinners arrive."

He scraped his chair legs back and stood. "After I visit the men's room."

Jace took the steps to the main floor and ambled past the porch railing behind the family, toward the restrooms.

A child's whimper drew Sydney's attention to the family. The mom strapped the wiggly little girl into a high chair. "Emily, what did I tell you before?" She signed the word "stay" and the child calmed. Then, as though sensing Sydney's stare, the child turned her head toward Sydney—which confirmed her suspicion. The girl had Down syndrome.

The little girl's face twisted.

Sydney signed, "Want play game?" then snatched a legal pad from her briefcase and held it in front of her face for a second before peeking around the tablet at the little girl. She hid behind the pad again, then pulled it down and made a funny face. The child giggled. Peekaboo always worked. The game continued until the child clapped and tried to copy Sydney's funny face. Sydney laughed out loud and signed "You funny."

The mother caught Sydney's eye and mouthed "Thank you," before putting a bib on her daughter. Sydney grinned and signed "You're welcome." Sensing that she was being watched, she lifted her gaze and spotted Jace behind the railing. How long had he been standing there?

Jace came around the railing and settled in his seat. "You are a woman of surprises. What else are you keeping from me besides knowing horses and being good at quieting fussy children with peekaboo games and sign language?"

She shrugged. "I did a lot of babysitting during high school. One of my charges had Down syndrome, and I learned some signs they used with her." *At least this time it's a true statement and not a lie.* "Shall we get back to what we were discussing? As I was saying, I made a bulleted list—"

Just then a waitress walked by with a platter of ribs. The smell of roasted meat and barbeque floated over her, and her stomach rumbled. Thanks to the children's noises, she doubted Jace noticed the embarrassing sound.

"It's difficult to hear you with those kids cutting up over there." Jace slid to a chair at a right angle to her. "If you want me to pay attention, I'm going to have to sit closer." Now he was near enough that she could smell his aftershave. She had to be strong and not let him know how close she was to giving in—to all the aromas wafting about from both man and beast.

Sydney pushed the iPad toward Jace and pointed at the screen. "Since they haven't yet paid you the full amount you agreed to, you have some wiggle room. That's good, because..." She looked up and her breath hitched. He'd leaned closer. So close that their lips were barely a kiss apart. Maybe he had given up his womanizing days, but he hadn't packed away his moves.

"Because what?"

Sydney inched away, her back straight. "I lost my train of thought."

He leaned back and set both forearms on the table. "Let me try. They haven't yet paid me the full, agreed-upon amount and that gives me some wiggle room. Which is good, because..." He leaned over and pushed a lock of hair away from her right cheek. "Your curls escaped your ponytail. It's cute that way."

She felt her spine relax. "I take it that's a compliment."

"At the highest degree." His gaze dropped to her mouth, and he leaned closer.

She wanted to move away, but her muscles were too busy tingling.

Was he going to kiss her right there? The last time she'd looked at the kids, they were coloring cowboy pictures the waitress had given them. They'd probably never notice. She closed her eyes and lifted her chin.

"I'd prefer to break the contract without paying them a dime. The time I've already given them more than compensates what they've paid me so far."

Sydney's eyes popped open. Jace was sitting back in his chair. Heat traveled up her neck, and she darkened the iPad. She wanted to toss her water at his irritating grin. "You will never negotiate a good settlement with that attitude."

"I'm used to battling." His grin dissolved. "I presume we're done with the business part of our evening."

"Not until we reach an agreement."

"I only said I'd discuss it tonight, and now we have. Do you want to catch a flick next door after we eat?"

She stuffed the tablet and folder into her briefcase. "You are impossible."

Jace sipped his sweet tea. "I thought you said I was incorrigible."

"That too."

"What do you say about the movie? I know it sounds like a date, but we can call it a couple of old friends hanging out."

Sharing an armrest for two hours in a dark theater sounded both frightening and wonderful. Sydney lifted her chin. "I've got work to do yet before lights out. I do have other clients."

He smirked. "Probably ones who pay a lot more than me."

"I'm sure the waitress would enjoy seeing a movie with you."

"That was a cheap shot. And here I thought you were a nice lawyer."

"I wasn't wearing my attorney hat when I said it." She laughed. "Here comes the food."

The waitress placed large platters on the table—prime rib for Jace and catfish for Sydney. When they were alone, he held out his hand. "Shall we pray?"

Sydney stared at his calloused palm. Did they need to hold hands? *This is praying, Sydney, not being romantic.* She rested her palm against his and he closed his fingers over hers. A delicious shiver raced up her arm.

"Heavenly Father, we thank you..."

His voice faded as a vision of living on his ranch as his wife and being able to work at the career she'd really wanted stole her attention. But "happily ever after" only happened in romance novels, not in real life. She'd learned that full well thanks to Logan Anderson and Ryan Kepler.

"Amen." Jace released his grip and she opened her eyes. He was already picking up his steak knife and cutting into his meal.

She cut off a piece of her fish with her fork, then lifted it to her mouth. Tasty enough, but she had a feeling Jace's tasted better. He hadn't spoken since he'd started working on that slab of beef. "How's your meat?"

He raised his head, his face a picture of bliss. "Incredible. Couldn't find prime rib any better in Texas."

Her mouth watered as he forked a bite of meat and put it into his mouth.

"How's your catfish?"

"Good."

"Just good?"

"That's right."

He forked another bite of the beef and held it out. "Try this. One little bite isn't going to cause the roof to fall in on you, is it?"

Sydney shook her head. The distinct aroma of prime rib was filling her senses. He was right. One little bite wouldn't hurt. She slowly opened her mouth, and Jace slid the forkful of beef inside. She closed her lips as he pulled the fork away. The beef seemed to almost melt on her tongue as memories of steak dinners Dad had made on the grill flooded her thoughts. She shut her eyes, as if that would help the bite and memory to stay with her. How had she let Ryan talk her into giving up something that evoked such happy memories?

"What do you think?"

Her eyes popped open. "I'd forgotten how good prime rib tasted. Thank you."

He grinned and cut an even larger hunk off his serving, placing it onto her plate. "It's a much larger serving than I need to eat. I'm happy to share."

An hour later they stepped outside, where a warm breeze caressed Sydney's face. If she went back to the hotel and worked, she'd probably be dead asleep in ten minutes. Maybe if she did what he wanted, he'd agree to renegotiate all the faster. After all, he'd shared half his prime rib with her. She stopped walking. "Wait. I've changed my mind. I'd like to see a movie."

7

Jace felt a grin stretching his face. The woman was a mystery, but he loved it. "You sure know how to surprise a guy." He glanced at the list of movies above the theater's entrance. Not many choices. An animated fairy tale? Nah. A thriller ... probably not Syd's favorite type of movie. A romantic comedy, likely a chick flick... The raunchy comedy probably had a lot of bad language. He'd leave the choice to her. "What's your pleasure?"

"The thriller is going to start in ten minutes. Let's go to that one."

He frowned. "Not the romantic comedy?"

She shook her head. "I'd rather have chase scenes and exploding helicopters than a sappy love story."

He shrugged. As he thought before—a mystery. Or was she just saying that because most guys would choose a shoot-'em-up over romance any day? "Let's do it."

They found their seats in the small theater as the last of previews and reminders to silence cell phones showed on the screen. Jace settled into his seat and glanced at the armrest that separated them. Did he let her have it and keep his hands in his lap or take half of it and try to avoid brushing her elbow? Hands in his lap seemed the best course.

An hour into the movie, Jace squirmed against the seat back. His favorite actors, favorite type of movie, and favorite way to relax and escape, but there was no way he could focus. Not with the intriguing and beautiful woman next to him. He hoped Syd wasn't the type to enjoy hashing out a movie after she'd seen it. He didn't want to admit his cluelessness about the plot.

Sydney shifted, and her head settled on his shoulder. He didn't move for the next ten minutes and neither did she. She had to be asleep, but how, with the amped-up noise of a chase scene rattling the walls of the small room? Using gentle movements, he extracted his cramped arm from beneath her and stretched it across her shoulders. She snuggled her head under his chin. Her familiar flowery scent drifted over him, and his pulse raced. Asleep or awake, he may as well enjoy the moment, because it might be the last time he'd be this close to her.

An hour later, the credits rolled across the screen and Jace heaved a sigh as he nudged Sydney into an upright position. "Syd, wake up. The movie's over."

She uttered a soft moan and yawned. "I fell asleep? Is the movie over? I'm sorry, Jace. I'm being lousy company."

"You slept through about half of the movie, but I was happy to provide my shoulder for a pillow." He moved his arm from behind her and worked it a few times to get the kink out.

She gathered her briefcase and purse from the floor. "The long drive and evening meal must have gotten to me. Did you enjoy the movie?"

"It was okay. Let's get out of here so you can get back to the hotel."

Jace stirred awake, confused. He was late, but where was he? His eyes opened and the sleep fog vanished. Syd was sleeping in what was to be his bed over at the hotel, and he was in the rig.

A vision of Syd's upturned face at the restaurant, her full lips slightly puckered in anticipation of his kiss, emerged into his thoughts. His hopes had ramped up when he saw she wanted him to kiss her, but not as much as they had later when she'd snuggled next to him in the theater. He'd have been more hopeful, though, if she'd done her snuggling while awake and not asleep. He had a feeling he'd missed one of her appealing blushes when she realized what she'd done. She'd barely spoken afterward, during the whole ride to the arena, and was probably chiding herself for cuddling next to him. He needed patience and lots of it.

Jace checked the clock on the truck's dash. Enough time to grab a shower and exercise Charley before his ten o'clock breakfast meeting with the rodeo kids' clinic committee to discuss his riding-and-roping class.

He reached for his cell phone and tapped on the direct number to her room. The ringtone sounded several times before she answered.

At her husky voice, a sinking feeling washed over him. "Hey, sounds like I woke you."

"What did you expect at six a.m.?"

"Seriously?"

"What time do you think it is?"

He checked his phone and put it back to his ear. "Syd, I'm sorry. The clock on the dash says eight. Call me when you're up."

"Dash?"

"Yeah, I'm sleeping on the bed in the truck cab. I let Clint have the bed in the trailer."

"Let me get coffee going and I'll call you back."

"Sure. Take your time." He disconnected and stared at the ceiling. "God, I don't want to go against Your will, but I need some time here. If she's the one for me, I don't want to blow it. Please, if stalling her isn't right, show me."

His phone rang, and he swiped a finger over the ACCEPT button. "Got the java going?"

"It's dripping into the pot. I miss my Keurig."

"Ah, we do have something in common."

"You have one too?"

"Yep."

They spent the next couple of minutes comparing which coffees they liked most. While they talked, Jace did his best to work himself into jeans and a T-shirt. He finished buckling his belt and took advantage of a pause in the conversation. "We should plan another meeting for this afternoon. What do you think?"

"You surprise me, Jace. I was sure I'd have to bring up our next appointment."

"There's a little town in Indiana with a nice park next to the river. It's about a half hour away. We can pick up some food and have our lunch while we talk." Where had that come from? He'd intended to suggest the restaurant next to her hotel. But a picnic sounded much more appealing.

Long silence filled the connection. "You make it sound like a date."

"So does dinner and a movie like we did last night. It's not like there are dozens of places around here to meet."

"True. What time should I pick you up?"

"How does noon sound? And I suggest you leave the high heels behind." He hoped the smile on his face came through the connection.

"I have to finish up some research for court on Tuesday. It will be done by then."

They ended the conversation, and Jace carried his boots and his Bible to the step outside the driver's door.

He'd just finished reading a chapter in Romans, the book he'd been working through the past several weeks, when the trailer entrance opened and Clint stepped outside, wearing jeans and no shirt. His long blond hair stuck out in all directions.

Jace snickered. " 'Bout time you got up."

Clint tugged a red PBR T-shirt over his six-pack abs and scratched his head. "It's not that late. You gonna work Charley this morning?"

"Plan to, before I meet Jeff Stahuley and his committee for breakfast. We need to fine-tune the kids' class for Saturday."

Clint sauntered over the grass, his flip-flops making a slapping sound against his bare feet, and sat next to Jace. "Maybe we can work with the roping dummy this afternoon."

"Don't you and the other bullfighters need to do your homework on tomorrow night's bulls?" Jace stuck his foot into a boot and tugged it on.

"We do, after they all arrive—which won't be until tomorrow."

"I have an appointment with my attorney today. It may take most of the afternoon."

Clint snickered. "A beautiful blond attorney, if I recall."

Jace slipped his other foot into the remaining boot, then stood and placed a Pioneer City Rodeo ball cap on his head. "Haven't noticed."

"I saw the cheesy grin on your face when she brought you back last night, McGowan. I haven't seen that expression on your mug in a long time."

"So what?"

"Didn't you say it was 'hands off' with her because she's a city girl?" He made air quotes as he spoke.

"People and situations can change."

Clint stood and leveled his gaze at Jace. "Dude, don't lose your head over this gal. You've only spent a couple of days together, and there's been *two years* between those days."

"I know, but our time earlier was a very long day and we had some deep discussions during those twelve hours."

Clint snickered. "Yeah, right. Discussions that involved some serious necking."

Jace grimaced. "I know that's how I was back then but, strangely enough, it wasn't like that with Syd. I kissed her, but not until we were saying good-bye at the end of the day. One kiss is all."

"If you're telling the truth, that must have been some kiss for you to remember it all this time. So, you guys picking up right where you left off?"

Jace studied the grass beneath his boots. He usually didn't keep much from Clint, but somehow, what was going on with Syd right then, he wanted to keep to himself. However, there was one thing he needed to discuss.

"She's let on that she's had some experience with riding but now she is afraid to get on a horse. I'm not sure why, but I've got a plan to help her with the fear."

Clint's expression grew serious. "You'd better be careful. Meddling with someone's emotional hang-ups can be chancy. What's the plan?"

"I'm gonna ask Lacy to work with Syd. Help get her back on a horse. Show her there's nothing to fear."

Clint shook his head. "What about her city ways? Ranch life doesn't mix well with skyscrapers."

"Just because I want to help her overcome her fear doesn't mean I'm lookin' to marry her." Jace walked to the back of the trailer, grabbed a feedbag, and filled it with Charley's special oat blend. He wasn't looking to marry Syd. Couldn't be. He recalled his prayer a while ago, asking God to show him if Syd were the one for him. God must have laughed at that request. They hardly knew each other, and no two people could be more opposite. But if he *were* looking, she ranked right up there as wife material.

8

Sydney turned into the arena and headed down the lane toward Jace's rig. Unlike yesterday, the rodeo grounds now bustled. Off to the right, people worked at setting up a carnival, while near the arena entrance, several men wearing baseball caps scurried around with clipboards.

The temperature had dropped into the more-comfortable eighties, and puffy cumulus clouds floated overhead.

A perfect day for a picnic with a handsome cowboy.

Her breath hitched as a warning bell sounded from a distant corner of her mind. This was a business meeting. Nothing more. A few hours for lunch and discussion, and she'd return to her hotel with Jace's agreement to renegotiate. If they ended early enough, she could start for Chicago this afternoon. She may not get home until after dark, but that would be okay.

Unbidden, memories of last night burst into her thoughts. When Jace jostled her awake at the end of the movie and she realized she was snuggled in his arm, she took a moment to come awake, not wanting to move. She'd let her guard down, and she couldn't let it happen again. She knew all too well how quickly those feelings of love and security could morph into rejection and hurt. She had to finish this assignment and leave as quickly as possible.

Sydney drove into the clearing beyond the arena. At least a dozen horse trailers and rigs filled the area, some with big semi-haulers like Jace's and others with large pickups. A couple of horses stood tethered to their trailers. In the open pasture, a woman rode a horse at an easy canter. The chestnut looked so much like Dad's horse, Prince, that tears pricked at the corners of her eyes, and she had to shake off the sorrow that hung over her like a dark cloud. She glanced off to her right.

Jace stood next to his rig wearing a blue shirt, his ever-present jeans, and boots. His Stetson had been replaced with a ball cap, giving him a boyish look. She drove his direction and parked a few feet away.

He sauntered over and climbed in, bringing his familiar woodsy scent with him. He flashed her a dimpled grin. "Good afternoon, Counselor." He ran his gaze over her. "Glad to see you've ditched the power suit. Jeans and sneakers are a much better choice. Did you have an enjoyable morning?"

Her hand went to her wavy ponytail, which cascaded down her shoulders. "Yes. I had time for a quick run and then I finished up what I was working on."

His brows arched. "You're a runner? How far do you usually go?"

"During the week, only two or three miles, depending on how soon I get up. On weekends, at least five when I run along the lakeshore path."

"Good to hear. I run three to five miles myself most days. But don't ask about today. Charley's the only one who ran this morning."

Fine. Another thing in common. "We all need a day off. Show me the way to Indiana." She gripped the gearshift handle.

Jace's hand landed on top of hers. "Not until you tell me why you're here when you have to be in court after the weekend. Shouldn't you have stayed in Chicago?"

She frowned. "What are you talking about?"

"You said you needed to have work done by Tuesday for a court case."

Loving his concern, she reluctantly tugged her hand from beneath his palm. "The case doesn't come up until Thursday, and only the lead attorney and his co-counsel will go before the judge. I'm a behind-the-scenes person. I sent my research to the lead attorney this morning before I came over here."

His brow furrowed. "I hear a tinge of disappointment in your voice."

She turned from his stare. Either she was a bad actor, or the man had ESP. The cowboy was too good to be true, and that was exactly why she needed to get out of Dodge ASAP. "I know I'm ready for a trial, but your uncle thinks otherwise."

"Did he promise you a promotion if I agree to negotiate?"

She snapped her gaze back to Jace. "What makes you think that?"

"I know my uncle pretty well and wouldn't put something like that past him."

"I'll move up at the right time." She reached over and turned on the radio. A lively instrumental tune burst through the speakers.

Jace directed her to a road that headed south, and a few minutes later they broke free from the confines of town. The two-lane road took them past farms and houses that sat on large lots and offered occasional glimpses of the Wabash River. Sydney cranked up the music. It had been a long time since she'd been in the country, and it felt wonderful. "Mind if I open the sunroof?"

He grinned. "Sounds good to me. I'll get it." He reached up and pressed a button. The small window slid open. Deep blue sky became their canopy, and a warm rush of wind filled the car, carrying with it the scent of freshly mowed grass.

Sydney lowered the windows. "I like to feel the wind in my hair. Not a convertible, exactly, but close."

Jace gave her a thumbs-up and tilted his seat back a notch.

The radio and wind noise put an end to all conversation, as Sydney had hoped. They were drifting into topics too personal for her comfort. She glanced at her passenger, loving that he felt comfortable enough to doze off while she drove. As if sensing her stare, his eyes opened and their gazes met. She jerked her focus back to the road.

A mile later, he snapped off the radio. "You're cute when you blush."

"I wasn't blushing."

"If it wasn't a blush, then you must have a sunburn." He reached over and touched her shoulder. "Admit it. You were blushing."

She shrugged his hand away. Staying neutral with him was impossible, especially when nearly everything he said seemed to showcase how right he was for her. But "right during the moment" didn't mean "right for life." She knew that full well. Except for being a man of faith, Ryan had ticked all the boxes too, and look how that had turned out. Never again would she be left at the last minute, having to explain to everyone that just hours before the wedding, her fiancé decided he loved another woman more. Jace now had a faith testimony, but there was that player reputation. Was his faith strong enough to keep him from relapsing?

Several minutes passed in silence. Jace's leather seat crackled as he repositioned himself. "Why are you so quiet?"

Sydney cast a quick sidelong glance his way. "You haven't exactly been vocal. I've been thinking about things. What's your excuse?"

"I've been thinking too—about the date we had two years ago. Best day of my life."

She tightened her grip on the wheel. He had to be exaggerating. "And how many women have you said that to in your lifetime?"

"Not many. Actually, maybe one other, and that was before I met you."

"I find that hard to believe."

"Look. I know I have a reputation as a ladies' man, or whatever you want to call it. But about 95 percent of what you hear isn't true."

"What about the 5 percent?"

"I've dated here and there, but what you hear has more to do with the buckle bunnies and those Frisky's ads. That's the brand they laid on me. I had nothing to do with it. And the sooner I'm done with them, the better." He crossed his arms and faced forward.

"Are 'buckle bunnies' the same as groupies?"

"Yep. They love all things cowboy and rodeo. They've zeroed in on me ever since the Frisky's sponsorship started. But I've never encouraged them. I dated a barrel racer from San Antonio for a while, but after I 'got religion'—her words, not mine—she broke it off. Even when we were going out, the dates with her never affected me the way our one day together did."

Sydney felt a smile working its way onto her face. The man had integrity even before he came to faith. She had to do her level best to help him get out of that contract in a way that didn't cost him the ranch. He didn't deserve any less than that. "The day felt like a fairy tale, didn't it? Perfect weather, great food, and…"

"A great kiss."

She jerked her gaze to her right and the car veered the same direction. She turned the wheel to the left and centered the car in the middle of their lane.

Jace released a low chuckle. "Good save. My fault for mentioning the elephant in the room while you're driving, but now that I have … I really wanted to kiss you last night to see if it would be the same."

"I'm glad you didn't, being that we were in the restaurant and all."

"Are you saying that if we were alone, it would have been okay?"

"That's a leading question."

"And you're avoiding an answer. You sure looked as if you wanted me to kiss you."

An uneasy feeling came over her. She had two choices: admit that in a weak moment she did want to feel his kiss again, or avoid the statement altogether—which was the same as admitting its truth. "I plead the Fifth."

He answered with a chuckle. "It took a lot of willpower not to follow through. I wasn't messin' with you. Just so you know. Wasn't the right moment."

Sydney took a deep breath. He was a keeper, and Erin would call her crazy for letting him get away. But Erin's love life was a perfect ten at the moment, and she couldn't expect her friend to understand.

"Syd, I'm not going to deny that the feelings I had for you back then haven't changed, and I sense you feel the same. What's so huge that it prevents us from seeing where we might go from here?"

She should tell him. But saying she'd been hurt before and couldn't bring herself to trust another man ever again sounded lame. People broke up with people all the time and eventually found others, so why couldn't she deal with it and move on?

"Syd?"

"I like you a lot, Jace, but there are reasons."

"Name one."

"As I said before, I want to carry on my dad's work, and I'll have more influence in the courts once I make partner."

"For what?"

"The legal clinic he started for addicts needs attorneys to work pro bono and help sway judges to send addicts to rehab, not prison. It's Dad's legacy, and once I've got some years under my belt, I'll be able to cut back on my hours at the firm and devote time to VLA. That's the clinic's name."

"Do you spend much time there now?"

"No, because your uncle has me billing a lot of hours, which translates into experience." She paused and looked at him. "For another reason, I've been raised in the city. It's where I belong."

"Were you living in the city when you used to ride horses?"

"Yes. Dad boarded his hor—" She drew in a breath and waited for the barrage of questions.

"Your dad had his own horse?"

"Yes, but I don't want to talk about it. Labor Day weekends are hard enough as it is." The road trip had lost its appeal. "How much farther is this park we're going to?"

"Not much. I'm sorry, Syd. I forgot about this being the anniversary of your father's death. I get it. I've got a lot of 'dad baggage' myself. The first anniversary of his death was hard on all of us, but I have to move past it for the sake of the ranch and my family."

Sydney tamped down the feeling of being chastened, certain Jace didn't realize how his comment came across. "I should be the one apologizing. I've had fourteen years since my dad's death, and the memory still unsettles me. Here, you've had only two."

"No need for apologies. My circumstances aren't the same, and we all react differently."

"The taxes. I know. How did he manage to mess up things so much?"

After a protracted silence, she glanced over. He'd crossed his arms and was staring out the side window. Now it was his turn to feel put on the hot seat. "I shouldn't have brought up the lien. I'm sorry."

"I don't want to drag my dad's dirty laundry into the discussion. It has nothing to do with my contract issues."

"Understood."

They came to a stop sign at a large highway. "Do I go left?"

"Yep. After we cross the river, we'll grab some carryout to take to the park."

Sydney made the turn, switched the radio back on, and let the music soothe the awkward silence. Maybe they could find a restaurant and pass on the picnic.

9

Thick woods lined the wide highway. As they headed down a hill, dark clouds swirled overhead, darkening the car's interior. Sydney lowered the radio volume. "Looks like bad weather. Maybe we should find a restaurant and eat inside." She shut the sunroof.

Jace peered through his window. "Those clouds are moving east at a pretty good clip. Looks clear back to the west. We're good."

By the time they crossed the Wabash River and entered Vincennes, Indiana, Jace's weather forecast had proven correct. They found a sandwich shop for carryout, then headed for the state park. Syd turned into the parking lot Jace directed her to and selected a space. Ahead of them, grass and trees spread out toward the river. A peaceful time next to water sounded perfect, but too many emotions had been stirred during the ride. What she needed was some alone time with God. Maybe, if he agreed to renegotiate without much discussion, they could have some personal space before heading back to the arena.

Sydney let Jace take the lead as they strode across the lawn toward the river. Off to the right, a large, white circular structure commanded a spacious grassy lawn. "Is that building a memorial?"

"Yeah. It's for George Rogers Clark. He defended a fort here against the Brits and saved it from being sacked. It's hard to imagine what the area was like back in the 1700s. About the only thing that hasn't changed is the river. Do you enjoy history?"

"I would if I had more time. My mom has uncovered some interesting facts about our ancestors by digging into musty courthouse records. The only courthouse records I get to see are current ones."

"My mom does that too. She's traced our family back several generations to when our ancestors first migrated from the east to the property that's our ranch today." His eyes clouded and he looked away.

Sydney ached for him. The man carried a huge load through no fault of his own.

They came to a picnic bench beneath a large oak tree, and Jace set the lunch bags on the table. He plopped onto the bench closest to the river, rested his back against the edge of the table, and then stared out at the water, his eyes still holding the hurt Sydney saw earlier.

She sat beside him. The slow-moving river should have brought her a calming effect, but with the tense man beside her, it wasn't working. "The ranch is more than just a piece of property, isn't it?"

His Adam's apple bobbed. "You got that right. And it all falls on me now. If we lose the ranch..." His eyes glistened and he blinked. "If I have to move my mom and kid brothers into a house in town ... I'll never forgive myself. I can't let that happen."

The unfamiliar huskiness in his voice struck a chord deep in Sydney's being. She lifted her arms, wanting to hug him as she would any close friend who was hurting, but then folded them across her chest. Oh, how she hated having to weigh her every move. "There's a lot on your shoulders with having younger siblings."

Jace scrubbed his face with his palms. "Yeah, I've tried to be a good role model to the twins, and that's another reason to separate from Frisky's."

"Will they stay on to help with the ranch after they finish high school?"

"Cole isn't into ranching much and will probably go into medicine like our older brother. But Tanner plans to stick around. He's become my right-hand guy. When Clint and I are on the rodeo circuit, he keeps the ranch running and me on speed dial."

"Older brother?"

Jace's lips flattened into a thin line. "Corey's a doctor in Colorado. No interest in the ranch at all. He actually suggested selling the property when Dad died. The rest of us were shocked when he said it. Then we learned about the tax thing, and he said no more. We have plenty of ranch help, so his noninvolvement isn't a problem. Clint lives on the ranch and works with Tanner. We also have a couple ranch hands who help, along with Lacy. She assists with the horses and cooking our main meal. We eat dinner at noon to fuel up for the afternoon work."

Sydney noticed a slight edge to his voice when he was talking about Corey that disappeared when he spoke about Clint and the others. It seemed Jace might not only have "dad baggage" but "brother baggage" as well. Sydney swallowed the temptation to use her cross-examination techniques. She wanted to dig more, but she'd avoid the subject today. "Do you all live together in the house?"

"For now. But I've started building my own place on the property. The outside is done and the inside is framed out, but its completion is on hold until this tax business is resolved." He faced her. "What about you? I don't remember your mentioning brothers and sisters."

Sydney looked away.

"From the face you just pulled, I think I struck a raw nerve."

She poked at a stick on the ground with her toe, then turned and met his gaze. She hated talking about her family. So many skeletons that it was hard to keep them all hidden. "I have an older brother. Nate was injured in a football accident during high school and has been a quadriplegic ever since."

The lines around Jace's eyes softened. "That bites. I'm sorry."

"It's been nineteen years since it happened, so I barely remember when he was able-bodied. He lives in his own house that students from the high school built for him and has round-the-clock help from several caretakers who work in shifts. He runs his own business from his house and even drives."

"High school kids built his house?"

"Every year, students in the trade classes take on building an actual house. Because my brother was injured at the school's football game, they decided to build one to accommodate him. It's not large, but it's more than adequate."

"That's cool. Do you see Nate often?"

An ache pressed against her chest. The same guilt she'd felt for years. "Not as much as I should." She looked over her shoulder at the lunch bags. "Shall we eat, so we can get to work?"

Jace swung his legs around and faced the table. "Good idea."

Sydney grabbed her bag and pushed to her feet.

He grasped her arm. "Where're you going?"

The feel of his palm against her bare skin burned like a hot iron. "To the other side. That way I can face you."

His dimples deepened. "I sure wouldn't complain if the lady shared my side of the table. I promise to keep a respectable distance."

Did he realize the strength of his smile? Of course he did, and he knew when to employ it. Well, this time it wasn't going to work. She tugged her arm from beneath his hand. "The lady prefers to sit across from you during the business meeting, which I hope we can start while we eat. Thanks anyway." Sydney moved to the other side of the table and pulled her sack containing a tossed salad with an add-on of chicken across the tabletop. She tore open the bag and spread it out to use as a place mat, then waited for Jace to unwrap his meatball sandwich.

He reached across the table and opened his hand. Sydney stared at the open palm. Prayer time. She never minded saying grace in public, but Jace's penchant to hold hands during prayer caused distractions that weren't exactly spiritual. It was best to keep her temporary client happy, though. She drew in a breath and let Jace take her hand. He wove their fingers together and squeezed. Butterflies danced in her stomach as she bowed her head, and his words faded as she lost herself in the warmth of his touch.

"Amen."

Sydney opened her eyes as their hands disconnected. Whatever he'd prayed, as always, she had no clue.

Jace unwrapped his sandwich, and the zesty aroma of ground beef, peppers, and spices drifted over to her. Memories of the meatball sandwiches she'd enjoyed in the past intruded on her thoughts. Finally freed of the conviction Ryan had instilled in her that red meat was never healthy, she'd been tempted to order a meatball sandwich for lunch herself but decided it was better to eat red meat in moderation. There was still dinner to be had before the day was over. She stabbed at her greens with her plastic fork and dipped them in the small cup of balsamic vinaigrette.

A distant train whistle and children's shouts behind them supplied background noise as they ate in silence. Over on the river, a motorboat puttered past with a lone driver at the wheel. Sydney yearned to cancel the business discussion ahead, but if she did, she'd have to spend another day in the cowboy's presence. Another day of temptation to throw caution to the wind and enjoy his company—and hold off the pangs of love that were mounting in her heart.

"Want some potato chips?"

Sydney eyed the open bag of chips Jace held out.

"Just one." She plucked one from the bag and put it into her mouth.

"Only one?"

"Anything is permissible in moderation." She offered a smile.

"I don't know what you're worried about. You aren't overweight. In fact, I think you're just right." He popped a chip into his mouth.

Grateful she didn't feel a blush at his compliment, Syd whispered a thank-you and reached for her briefcase. Back to reality, and the sooner the better.

10

Jace stifled a yawn. Keeping his eyes on Syd was never a problem, but listening to the litany he'd heard a zillion times was harder than roping a frisky calf. Especially when he really did agree with her. Was he crazy to keep her dangling? Lacy would arrive tomorrow, and she'd promised to work with Syd and what Jace supposed was some irrational fear of horses. One more day. He had to hang on only one more day.

Sydney waved her tablet in front of his face. "Earth to Jace, come in, please."

He blinked. "I'm listening."

She rolled her eyes, causing her long lashes to sweep upward over her lightly tinted lids. "You probably didn't hear a single word I said."

"Wrong, Counselor. I need to protect my reputation and renegotiate. If I break the contract, I may destroy all my chances for new sponsors."

"I said that fifteen minutes ago. What I *last* said was that if you don't agree to renegotiate, Frisky's will have every right to tie you up to a fence post in a round pen filled with mountain lions."

He removed his cap and ran his hand through his hair. "You didn't really say that."

She crossed her arms and frowned. "What I don't understand is why you won't renegotiate, when you need every dollar possible for those taxes."

He grabbed his phone from where it lay on the table and checked the time. They had a good hour before they needed to head out, and he didn't want to spend the time rehashing everything.

"You must have a secret stash somewhere you've not mentioned."

Jace rested his elbows on the table and leaned toward Syd. Their gazes met, and he had to work to not get lost in her mesmerizing stare. "I have a proposition to make."

A blond brow arched. "Why do I feel as if I'm about to be played?"

"It's all good. I've learned that the best way to work through fears is with prayer and facing those fears head-on. My cousin Lacy arrives tomorrow. You said that getting on a horse again scares you. I asked Lacy, if you were willing, to work with you while I'm teaching the kids' clinic on Saturday morning. To help you overcome your fear."

The same brow arched again and she stiffened. "I didn't say I was afraid. What did you tell her?"

"Sure you did. When I was surprised that you recognized the brand of treats I feed Charley, you said the idea of getting on a horse again scares you."

She swallowed hard and looked past him. "I guess I did say that. What else did you tell your cousin?"

A lump that felt like a hard rock formed in his throat. "Not much. Only asked her if she'd have time to work with a friend of mine on riding Saturday morning."

"I told you I wasn't planning to stay long. If you agree to renegotiate today, I'll be on my way home by tomorrow morning."

Jace leaned back. He was going to lose her if he didn't say his words right. "You don't want to be able to enjoy horseback riding again?"

Moisture glistened on her lashes. "I'm not sure."

Time to go for the real reason behind all this. "How did your dad die, Syd?"

She turned away. "In a horse accident."

Bingo. "What happened?"

She turned back to face him and drew in a deep breath. "Dad's horse spooked and threw him. His head hit a rock. He died almost instantly."

Jace wasn't expecting that. If her dad died fourteen years ago, she would have been a teenager—about as old as his twin brothers when their dad died. He'd change the subject, but this might be the last chance to have the discussion. He had to choose his words carefully. He made an effort to soften his voice and said, "Are you afraid of being thrown the same way?"

Syd shook her head. "I don't think so." She shot him a skeptical look. "Why Lacy? Why not you?"

"I thought it would be better if a woman helped." Across the grassy carpet, a couple of squirrels chased each other up a tree. If Syd agreed to his plan, it would buy him one more day to keep her there. "There's more."

She lifted her gaze toward the sky. "Ah, now comes the catch."

"If you can ride a horse for five minutes, I'll agree to renegotiate. If you can't, then I head to Arkansas on Sunday as planned and you return to Chicago. You'll still be home in time to spend Labor Day with your mom. I'll make sure Uncle Harry understands that you did your best."

She drew in another long breath and closed her eyes. One minute stretched into two. If she didn't say something soon, he—

She opened her eyes. "Five minutes is all?"

"Yep. Five minutes."

"Okay. I'll do it."

Grinning, he stuck out his hand. "Shake on it?"

She nodded.

He took her outstretched hand and wove their fingers together. She didn't pull away, which surprised him. It seemed so natural to be holding hands with her. A warm sensation came over him. "Your hand fits nicely in my big ol' mitt."

"I plead the Fifth."

He rubbed his thumb over the back of her hand—skin so soft, he feared his calluses would cut it. She didn't resist. Did he dare do what he'd wanted to do since that day at Malnati's? He leaned across the table until they were eye-to-eye, inches apart. "Shall we seal the deal?"

"Isn't that what we're doing with the longest handshake in history?"

"That's only half the way it's done."

"I'm afraid to ask what the other half is."

With his free hand, he trailed his index finger down her cheek, then ran its tip around her full mouth. She didn't resist. He leaned closer. She remained still. Would it be like last time? His mouth found hers. Lips soft against his. Kissing him back. Heaven. Her hand went to his neck and drew him closer. A tiny moan came from her throat.

The kiss ended, and he kept his gaze locked on hers as he leaned away far enough to see her beautiful face. Crazy as it seemed, he was falling in love with her. And here he thought people only fell in love that fast in movies. Did she feel the same? *Give me one hint.*

A smile lit her face. "Wow."

His heart rate quickened, and he took both her hands in his. "Much better to stop resisting, don't you think? Maybe we're meant to—"

"Don't say it." She placed her index finger over his lips.

Jace kissed her finger, then slid off the bench and came to her side. He sat beside her and circled her small waist with one arm. She leaned into him, laying her head against his chest. He nuzzled his nose into her hair, breathing in its flowery scent. She was intoxicating.

They sat quietly as a soft breeze curled around them. Overhead, a bird tweeted. *A perfect day.* He pressed a kiss to the top of Sydney's head. If only he could bottle the moment and take it back to Texas. "What are you thinking about, Syd?"

She leaned back enough that she could look at him. "I have strong feelings for you, Jace, but you have your life in Texas and I have mine in Illinois."

She wasn't getting off that easy. Jace released her and stood. "Let's walk to the river." He grabbed her briefcase and handed her purse to her. "We'll take these with us."

Syd slid the purse strap over her shoulder and kept her arms folded across her chest as they strolled side by side to a sun-splashed patch of lawn. If only he could read her mind. A fear of horses and carrying on her dad's desire to help addicts were viable reasons but not obstacles that couldn't be overcome. What else was holding her back?

He tossed his jacket onto the grass next to a maple tree. "Have a seat."

Sydney dropped to the makeshift blanket. She faced the river, stretched out her legs, and leaned against the tree trunk.

He lowered her briefcase to the ground, then sat beside her. "Don't you love a slow-moving river? Reminds me of the song about the 'Old Man River that just keeps rolling along.' "

"All we have at home is the Chicago River, and it's never lazy. I could get used to this."

"We have a river on the ranch. It's my favorite place to think and pray."

"Sounds lovely. It's nice to be close enough to Lake Michigan that I can go over there to run. But it's rarely quiet enough to sit and reflect."

He moved around until he faced her, crossing his legs Indian-style to bring his head close to hers. He looked her in the eyes. "What's eating you, Syd?"

"What do you mean?"

"I have a hunch there's more you're not saying. If you tell me the real reason we can't start a long-distance relationship and see where it goes, I'll go away."

Her chin trembled, and she stared at her lap.

Great. He wanted to take her into his arms and comfort her, but maybe it wasn't a good idea. He never did well with women and tears. *Best let her make the first move.*

Sydney raised her gaze, her eyes sad but dry. The tremble was gone. He inched closer and waited. She didn't move. He returned to her side and gathered her into his arms. She didn't resist.

He'd stay there as long as she wanted. Jace brought his hand to her hair and tugged at the elastic until her waves spilled over her shoulders.

"I thought you liked my hair pulled up."

"I do, but free around your face is best. It feels so soft—and smells good too."

"Your words make all the money I spend on hair products worth it." She snuggled closer. "I can hear your heart beating."

"It must be racing at warp speed."

"It is pretty fast, but so is mine."

"Then we're a good match." He leaned back and tipped her chin upward with the crook of his finger. Did he dare say what was on his heart? "Can we at least agree to that?"

"Agree to what?"

"That we're a good match."

She dropped her gaze, and her lashes grazed the tops of her cheeks. "Good matches don't always mean good for a relationship."

"You are about as stubborn as me. But stubbornness begs to be broken in." He leaned in and brought his lips to hers. He'd never tasted lips so soft, so wonderful. He pulled back and kissed her nose and closed eyelids before running a trail of feathery kisses around her face until she let out a gentle sigh. "And this is a reason we're good together," he whispered. "We have kissing to look forward to when we lock horns."

"I know, but we can't always be locking horns. At some point someone will say enough is enough and..."

"And what?"

"You know."

He kissed her again. "All I know is that I'm crazy about you and I'll never say enough is enough."

She wriggled free of his embrace and put more space between them. "The less we talk about that, the better." She moved to stand.

Jace grabbed her by the hand. "Why can't we talk this out?"

She settled back on his jacket but didn't look at him. "Because every time we do, we end up kissing. There's a lot more to a good relationship than the physical."

He let out a *whoosh* of air. If patience was a virtue, he was soon going to be the most virtuous man around. "You don't think I know that? There's a million reasons I care for you besides the physical."

"And I can say the same about you." She shot to her feet and picked up her bags. "We're in a bubble right now, not in our real worlds. It's best to keep that in perspective. Let's head back to the arena." She slipped the carrying straps of her briefcase and purse over her shoulder and started walking toward the car.

Jace scrambled to his feet and grabbed his jacket. He was frustrated with her refusal to talk, but at least she'd agreed to the challenge and he was assured of another day.

A few moments after passing the WELCOME TO ILLINOIS sign, Sydney turned onto the road back to Palestine. They hadn't said much since they'd left the park, and she'd spent most of the drive so far asking herself what she'd been thinking by agreeing to the inane idea of riding a horse to get him to renegotiate. But if that's what it took, so be it. She touched her lips with her fingertips. The cowboy sure knew how to kiss. She hated the earnest look on his face in response to what she'd said after their last kiss. The past couple of days with Jace had been magical, to say the least, just as their day together was two years ago. But she knew how it worked. They'd get back to normality, she in Chicago and he in Texas, and the magic would fade. Next, she'd hear he'd met someone along the way. They'd kissed just a few times since she'd arrived, but every time they did, the resolve to not give away her heart waned a bit more.

She glanced at Jace. He'd reclined the seat and fallen asleep. The cap bill angled off toward the window, giving her a hint of how he must have looked as a child, minus the stubbled jaw. Her heart squeezed and she forced her eyes back to the road. *Admit it, Sydney. You're falling big-time.* Falling for his charms, his wit, his integrity … everything about him.

She snapped on the radio harder than necessary and did a search with the scanner until it landed on a country music station. Probably Jace's music choice anyway. She left it there. Anything to get her mind to think about something other than all the reasons he was good for her.

"Want to get together later for dinner?"

She started and looked over at him. "I thought our business meetings were over until the horse ride."

He raised his seat to the upright position. "I wasn't thinking about a business dinner. I was thinking about having an enjoyable meal with a special woman. What most people call a date."

She couldn't get the words out to decline, and they rode the rest of the way in silence, each in their own thoughts.

At the arena, she drove down the lane and parked near the rig.

Jace faced her. "You never answered my question."

"I'd like to have dinner, but I really shouldn't."

"Shouldn't, or can't?"

"I meant *shouldn't*, but *can't* would be a better word. That work we talked about before."

"The court deal. I thought you sent that off this morning."

"I always have work to do. It never ends."

"No problem. Clint and I can grab something. He's not as pretty as you, but he's good company."

A lump rose in her throat. She hadn't expected him to give in so fast, and now she really hated going back to the hotel with a long night stretched out ahead of her—alone. "I'm glad you have a good friend in Clint."

"Yeah. Me too." Jace gripped the door handle but didn't move to open it.

Sydney put the car in REVERSE. "I need to get going. I'll see you on Saturday morning."

His eyes widened. "And not come to the rodeo tomorrow night? I got you VIP seats right next to the chutes." He pointed toward the arena. "See those steps going up to that covered platform? You'll be as close to the action as possible without being on the dirt."

She returned the gear shift to NEUTRAL. "Oh. I hadn't even thought about the rodeo. It would be nice to see you ride."

He gave her a playful punch in her arm. "That's better. You have all day to work. Be at the arena no later than six. I'll let the gate know you're my guest, and they'll let you come down the lane to the rig."

"Sounds like a plan, cowboy." She raised her palm and he high-fived her.

A grin split his face, and the dimples became deeper than ever. He glanced into the back seat. "You still have Lacy's boots. Wear 'em when you come. No high heels allowed. I'll call you in the morning. Have a good night." He leaned over and stole a quick kiss, then climbed out of the car and shut the door.

She didn't back up until he'd walked halfway toward the pens and turned to wave.

Sydney's insides felt as if they'd turned to mush. "God, why can't things be different?"

11

Jace stood beside the rig as a red Ford truck with Texas plates hauled a horse trailer up the lane. As the vehicle neared, Lacy leaned her head through the open passenger window, her long blond hair lifting in the stiff breeze, and waved. The truck rolled to a stop, and Jace trotted up to the driver's side.

Rob Elliott, one of the season's best steer wrestlers, rolled down his window. "Where should I park?"

Jace pointed toward the empty patch of grass the other side of the rig. "Right there next to me. Ready to wrestle some steer tonight?"

Rob yawned. "After I get some shut-eye. We drove all night. I should say *I* drove all night. Your cousin over there got her beauty sleep."

Lacy gave him a friendly punch in the arm. "I offered to drive, but oh no. A girl couldn't possibly drive this thing and do it right. Like I never haul around a horse trailer." She laughed, then opened her door and jumped out.

She rounded the front of the truck, and Jace met her with a hug. "Good to see you, cuz."

Lacy laughed. "We only saw each other a week ago. We live together, remember?"

"For as much as we're together when we're both there. We're usually like two ships passing in the night."

Lacy nodded. "But I always know you've been there when I see that the freezer needs restocking with my exceptional cooking."

While they talked, Rob put the truck and trailer in motion and drove toward where Jace had directed. Jace turned from watching Rob and faced Lacy. "I've got Charley in the pen on the other side of my bulls." He gestured with his thumb in the direction of the animals. "Go ahead and put Shiloh and Rob's horse in with Charley, and then I want to talk to you."

"About the lawyer gal you mentioned?"

He rested his hands on his hips and stared at the ground. "Yeah, about that. Her daddy was killed when his horse threw him. I'm almost certain his accident triggered her fear of getting back in the saddle. I've seen her look at Charley with longing. I'd like for her to enjoy riding again."

Lacy crossed her arms and grinned. "You sure she's not looking at you instead of your horse? I've seen that look on a few buckle bunnies when they stare at you."

Jace huffed a breath. "Come on, Lacy. You know that most of what you hear is all rumor."

"Maybe your being a player is a rumor, but the longing looks sent your way aren't."

He shrugged. "Can we get back to what we were talking about? Just help me out. Syd's a great gal, and I want to do this for her." He hated how his voice broke.

Her brows rose into a pair of perfect arches. "Wow, that's a lot of emotion I hear. You sure Sydney's not more than a friend?"

Lacy knew him too well. But he wasn't ready to talk about his feelings for Syd. Not as long as she insisted that they were all wrong for each other. He pushed his cap back on his head. "That's not why I'm doing this. Go on and get Shiloh settled."

Lacy looked toward the pasture. "I'd like to take her on a couple of laps before putting her in the pen. Why don't you saddle Charley, and we can talk while we ride?"

By the time Jace rode Charley over to the pasture, Lacy and her horse trotted along the far side of the field. "Come on, boy, let's catch up." He nudged Charley with his heels and made a clicking sound. The horse sped up and, within a few moments, they came alongside Lacy. The horses greeted each other, rubbing noses and nickering.

"Shiloh's glad to see her old friend." Lacy grinned. "Maybe you should keep Charley home more often. They may make some beautiful babies."

Jace threw back his head and laughed. "Always the romantic, aren't you?"

"I've got to look for it elsewhere since nothing much is happening in my life. So am I going to meet Sydney before our lesson?"

"She's doing some lawyering work at the hotel right now, but she'll be at the rodeo tomorrow night. I managed to grab a few seats in the VIP section. That way, when I'm not competing, I can sit with her and explain things. Maybe you could pop up there early and let me introduce you."

"Sounds good. Which horse am I to use to teach her?"

"Since Shiloh is a little more docile, maybe she should ride her. I'll need Charley for the first half of the clinic I'm teaching. As soon as we finish the riding portion, you can take Charley."

"Okay."

"There's something else. I told Sydney that she only needs to ride for five minutes."

"That's a short time. What happens if she rides that long? She gets you as the prize?" Lacy's eyes twinkled.

"Very funny. She's here to convince me that I should renegotiate the Frisky's contract and not just quit it like I said I was going to do. I told her, if she made it for five minutes, I'd renegotiate."

Lacy glared at him. "Jace, this isn't a joke. I thought by now you'd have come to your senses. What are you waiting for? Let me spell it out for you: T–A–X–E–S."

Jace held up a hand. "I do intend to renegotiate. I have my reasons for not telling Sydney until after the challenge."

"I don't like this one bit, and I have half a mind to step away from this scheme. You only just met and you're messin' with her. If she ever finds out the truth, you can kiss any chance of dating her good-bye."

"I didn't just meet her, Lacy. We met two years ago."

She cast him a skeptical look. "Really? Why haven't you mentioned her before?"

"Let's stop for a minute." Jace directed Charley to the side of the pasture and halted the horse. To his relief, Lacy came with him. They positioned the horses side by side. He didn't like confiding his feelings about Syd to his cousin, but he needed to make sure she understood that his intentions were genuine.

Lacy twisted in the saddle, the leather creaking as she faced Jace. "Okay, tell."

"We met when I visited Uncle Harry two years ago. Sydney works for him, and when he had something come up, he asked her to show me around the city. We hit it off and spent the whole day together. By the time the day ended, we both agreed we had a strong connection, but she insisted we weren't a good match. That she had to stay in Chicago to carry on her deceased father's law work ... and, of course, with the ranch and all, I can't leave Texas. I never mentioned it because the whole thing ended before it ever began."

"So how did she end up back in your life?"

"You know how I was at first, blowing off my mouth, saying I was going to quit Frisky's no matter what the contract said. Mom insisted I talk to Uncle Harry on my way here from Wisconsin. I intended to tell him that I already planned to negotiate a cancellation, but before I could, he sent Sydney and me out to lunch so she could knock sense into my head."

Lacy climbed off Shiloh and ground-tied the horse. "Let's sit. Easier to talk."

Jace got Charley settled a short distance from Shiloh and joined his cousin where she sat on the grass.

She stretched out her legs and crossed them at the ankles before leaning back on her arms. "I surmise the spark you two had a couple of years ago reignited over that lunch?"

"Yeah. So I decided to play along to see where our relationship may go. When she hadn't succeeded in convincing me to renegotiate, Harry sent her down here." He chuckled. "She thought she'd only be here one night and I'd cave."

"Like I said, you're messing with her. If she really had feelings for you, Jace, nothing would stop her from wanting to be with you."

"If I thought she didn't have feelings for me, I'd stop this nonsense so she could leave. I think she's scared of our getting involved, and I don't know why. I've decided to give it till Saturday, and if nothing changes, then so be it."

"Hence the challenge."

"Yep." He hated that the setup sounded manipulative, but it was his last hope.

"Okay, but if I find out after I get to know her that she truly has no interest in you, my participation is over."

He drew in a breath. "I guess if I'm not reading her right, I need to know the truth. Thanks." He moved to stand.

"Before we remount, you need to know something, Jace."

He tensed. The last time he saw that serious expression on her face was when she told him a prize heifer needed to be put down. "What's wrong?"

"Cole's in trouble."

"Cole? Not Tanner?" His twin brothers had been good kids and good students, but ever since Dad died, Tanner's grades had fallen off and he had gotten mixed up with a bad crowd. A few times in detention had cured him of his troubles, and he'd poured himself into ranch work ever since, when he wasn't in school.

"Cole and a couple of other kids got involved in some serious pranking last week."

"And I wasn't told?"

"Your mom didn't tell you because you have a lot on your mind already, and she didn't want to upset you."

"What happened?"

Lacy stared off at nothing for a second, as if trying to gather the right words. "Some kids decided to let the air out of the school buses' tires. All eighteen buses were disabled last Friday and school had to be called off. It's a breaking-and-entering case because they broke the lock on the bus barn to get in."

He winced. "I can't picture Cole doing something like that."

"He was the lookout in front of the school. But all the kids were lumped together. They're expelled for three days and have to do thirty days of community service. Cole will miss the season's first rodeo since he's scheduled to help at a homeless shelter the same day."

Jace scratched his head. "I thought Cole had a brain."

"He does, but he's still a kid, and kids want to fit in."

"How did my mom take it?"

"Not well. Jace, she needs you home more."

His stomach churned and bile rose to his throat. He couldn't be at the ranch more when being on the road meant more money coming in. He pulled his cell phone from his pocket and stabbed at his brother's name on the contact list. "I'll give him a call and see what I can do from here."

Sydney spooned the last of her yogurt into her mouth and swallowed the peachy goodness. At least her stomach had settled overnight, and for that, she was grateful. She sat the empty container on the side table, then leaned against the soft couch cushion and pulled her computer onto her lap. Her cell rang and she jumped, surprised to hear a call coming through. She checked the screen, then swiped the ACCEPT prompt.

"Hi, Harry."

"Sydney, if I didn't know better, I'd think I was being avoided. I called you yesterday and never heard back."

"Sorry. My cell service doesn't cover this area and the signal is spotty. It's best to try the hotel landline if I don't pick up. Jace still hasn't agreed to renegotiate, but I'm working on him."

"How much time have you been able to spend with him?"

"Enough. Yesterday we took a side trip to a small town in Indiana. I thought that if we could get away from everything rodeo for a while, we'd get somewhere with the negotiating."

"And did you?"

"Sort of."

"What does that mean?"

"He insists on my doing something, and if I do it, then he'll agree to renegotiate."

"You're not making sense."

She drew in a long breath and held it.

"Syd, talk to me. What is he asking you to do?"

"He wants me to take a horseback-riding lesson from his cousin. If I can stay on for five minutes without getting scared, he'll renegotiate."

"That's the most ridiculous thing I've ever heard. Why does he think you're scared to ride a horse? You're as good a rider as he is."

"You know I haven't ridden a horse since Dad died."

"I didn't know."

Sydney clenched her jaw and mentally started counting. She didn't speak until she arrived at eight. "You did, Harry. I've told you countless times."

"I don't remember. Well, it must be like riding a bicycle. Once you learn, you never forget. Why haven't you ridden?"

Did she really want to talk about this with her boss? "I have my reasons. But it will please you to know that for the sake of getting him to renegotiate the cancellation, I'm going to tough it out and get on a horse."

"That's a girl."

She could hear the smile in his voice. At least one of them was happy.

"When is this ride supposed to happen?"

"Tomorrow morning. Lacy is supposed to work with me." She hesitated. "I'm hoping to be on the road back to Chicago by the afternoon."

"Well, Lacy does have an easy way about herself, just like her mother."

They went on to discuss the other case Sydney was working on and hung up afterward. She tossed the phone onto the cushion next to her. Tears stung her eyes. After tomorrow, it would all be over. Five minutes—probably two laps around the pasture—and she'd be free to head home and back to the not-so-exciting life of a big-city lawyer.

Jace would eventually find someone, and she'd soon be forgotten. It was bound to happen, no matter what she decided as far as Jace was concerned. She smiled at the memory of hearing Jace's joy over the phone earlier when he'd called to be sure she hadn't changed her mind about attending the rodeo. She wanted to say that she couldn't wait to see him ride his bull and to cheer him on, but it would only encourage him.

Sydney went to the tub and turned on the water. She might as well have another turn with the jets before getting ready for the rodeo. Going home meant she'd be back to her small tub and only memories of the past few days.

She squirted in scented bath gel and went to the closet to pick out an outfit. Jeans were a given, along with Erin's boots and shirt—she'd return Lacy's boots tonight.

A few minutes later, she slid into the tub and switched on the jets. Pulsing hot water pounded at the small of her back. Sydney closed her eyes and leaned her head against the waterproof pillow the hotel had provided. She smiled and touched her fingertips to her lips. Two kisses yesterday—three, if she counted the quick good-bye kiss—and one two years before. Not much to go on, but she'd definitely fallen for the man. Not only because of his kisses, either, but because of the man he'd become. A good man. A man who ticked all her boxes. A man's man—and yet he could be tender at the same time.

Erin would help her sort out her thoughts. She grabbed a fluffy washcloth from the supply on the edge of the tub and began scrubbing her face. If she hurried, she could get in a call to her friend and still have time to dress for the rodeo.

Relieved her cell still had a signal, Sydney listened to the ring sound in her ear and prayed Erin would pick up.

"Hey, girlfriend, how's life at the rodeo?"

Prayer answered. "Depends on how you look at it."

"No success on Jace agreeing to renegotiate?"

"Yes and no."

"Okay. And how is it spending your days with that hunk of a cowboy?"

Heaven. But did she really want to admit to Erin her true feelings? If she did, she'd never hear the end of it when she came home. What was she thinking, wanting to confide in Jace's most ardent fan?

"Syd, you still there?"

"We have bad cell service down here. You cut out."

"I asked how things were going with the hunk."

"If you are inferring that I should be head over heels for the guy by now, how could I be attracted to someone who lacks common sense?"

A soft chuckle came through the line. "I may be mistaken, but it seems you are protesting a tad too much. I'm your best friend. You can tell me. Isn't the first rodeo tonight?"

"It is. In fact, I need to hang up and get dressed in those wonderful clothes you loaned me."

"Then why did you call?"

"Just wanted to touch base and let you know I'll likely be home by tomorrow sometime. I'll call when I get there."

They said their good-byes and Sydney disconnected. Good thing she came to her senses. Some things were just better left unsaid.

12

Sydney followed a Ford Explorer into the arena grounds, and a uniformed officer signaled her into a line of cars snaking toward the general parking lot. She lowered her window and called out, "Jace McGowan, one of the bull riders, arranged for me to drive to where his rig is parked. My name is Sydney Knight." She handed him her driver's license when he came to the window.

The officer studied the license and went to the front of the Prius. He glanced at her license plate, then checked something on a clipboard before he returned to her window and handed back her ID. "Enjoy the rodeo."

Feeling like a VIP, Syd waved her thanks and proceeded down the lane.

Jace waited next to the pens. His plaid long-sleeved shirt, jeans, and boots fit him perfectly, as always. He ambled over, bringing his dimpled smile with him, and her stomach dipped. She lowered her window. "Sorry I'm a little late."

"I was beginning to wonder if you weren't on the list. I called it in this morning."

"My name was there. No problem." Sydney climbed out of the car. A happy tune drifted over from the carnival, bringing with it a memory of riding on a carousel pony with Dad standing next to her, his strong arm around her waist.

"Syd, you okay?"

She snapped her attention to Jace. "I'm fine."

"Good. For a minute there, you seemed a million miles away."

She glanced around. Several cowboys in conversation hung out near the pens, while bulls trotted down a ramp from the back end of a truck and into a corral. In the arena, a tractor pulled a contraption back and forth over the dirt.

She smiled at Jace. "The place is buzzing."

"It's rodeo time. Lots of energy."

Syd turned away from the grin that had overtaken his face and looked off into the distance. "If you don't get rained out. The sky to the west looks threatening."

"Doesn't matter. We rodeo anyway."

"Even in a thunderstorm?"

"Most of the time."

"Is that safe? So much around here is metal—even the stands. And the animals could lose their footing." She couldn't help but express concern.

"Is bull riding safe?" A deep *V* formed between his eyes. "You afraid of storms?"

"Not usually."

He looked over her shoulder and raised his arm in a wave. "Here comes my cousin."

Sydney turned. A tall young woman wearing jeans and a blinged-out, long-sleeved purple shirt strolled toward them. Long blond waves flowed from under her Stetson and down her back. Beside her, a man wearing a brown Stetson, clownish shorts, and a sports jersey walked beside her.

Jace grinned at the pair. "Sydney Knight, this is Lacy Roberts, my cousin, and Clint Palmer, one of the bullfighters and my right-hand man on the ranch."

Lacy stuck out her hand. "Glad to meet you, Sydney. I hear we're going to have some fun tomorrow on the horses. Do you prefer *Syd* or *Sydney*?"

Sydney loved Lacy's friendly manner and the twinkle in her eyes. Maybe tomorrow wouldn't be so bad after all. That is, if she passed the inspection Lacy was giving her with eyes almost the same deep blue as Jace's. "Either name is fine. I'm looking forward to it. I think."

Lacy let out a guffaw and gave Jace a playful punch in the arm. "What are you telling her, cuz? Don't believe a word he said, Sydney. I'll join you in the stands before I have to prep for my race."

"Looks like we'll both be with you for a while," Jace said. "The barrel racing and bull riding come at the end of the competition. Three seats were available, so I snagged 'em."

Clint looked at Jace. "I'll see you behind the chutes." He next focused on Sydney. "Nice to meet you, Sydney. Enjoy the rodeo."

Sydney returned the sentiment and watched Clint until he disappeared from view somewhere between the pens and the back side of the chutes. She focused on Jace and Lacy. "Don't feel you both have to sit with me on my account. I imagine you have a set routine before you have to ride that doesn't include sitting in the stands."

"I'll leave in plenty of time to prep. Rodeos can be confusing for a newbie," Jace said. "With us there, you won't be so lost."

He had a point. Although she was somewhat familiar with barrel racing, the other events left her in the dark. She'd intended to research them but had gotten caught up in working on a brief. She checked the sky. Already the ominous clouds were breaking up.

She smiled at Jace. "You're right. Any help I can get is welcome."

A country-western tune blasted through overhead speakers affixed to the building behind the chutes. Not usually her music of choice, but any other kind would not have fit the scenario. She glanced at Jace's bulls still in the pen behind them. "When do your bulls get moved?"

"Not for a while. The broncs and mutton-bustin' have reservations in the chutes before them."

Sydney quirked her head. "Mutton-bustin'?"

"Oh, Sydney, wait till you see it." Lacy's grin matched the excitement in her voice. "Little kids are put on the backs of sheep and the sheep take them for a ride." She frowned briefly. "You can wipe that worried look off your face. They wear helmets, and they only run a short ways before they fall off. No winners. Everyone gets a prize."

"Fall off? Helmets protect their heads, but what about the rest of them?"

Jace laughed. "The sheep are only a couple of feet high. The kids probably fall farther while playing at home or at school."

A baritone voice spoke over the country music, announcing that the rodeo would begin in a half hour, so the threesome started walking the short distance to the VIP section.

Jace stepped over to a wiry guy who looked like he was barely out of his teens. "Hey, Tyler. Good to see ya again."

The man looked up from running his gloved hand over a rope tied to the fence rail. "I wasn't sure I'd make it this year. Got a concussion in late July and didn't get the okay to ride until last weekend. This is my first time using a helmet. It's gonna take some getting used to."

"I know what you mean. I tried using a helmet once and went back to not using one. God's got my back." Jace looked at Sydney. "This is Sydney Knight, and I think you already know my cousin, Lacy."

Tyler nodded at Sydney. "Good to meet you, ma'am. I hope you enjoy the rodeo."

The polite tone of voice mixed with a Southern accent similar to Jace's Texas one impressed Sydney. "I'm sure I will. Thanks, Tyler."

The threesome continued toward the seats. Jace had spoken so casually about not using a helmet. No doubt God wanted Jace to trust Him, but He didn't mean for him not to use the brain He'd given him too.

They arrived at the metal stairs leading to the VIP section. Off to the right and running along the arena's length, people were filing into a long bank of metal bleachers. Some wore Stetsons and boots, and others wore shorts and sandals, which made more sense given the warm evening. Already, Sydney's feet felt as if they were smothering in the socks and leather boots.

Jace followed Sydney up the steps to the platform. Tucked against the red bucking chutes, the covered platform held only two rows of cushioned wood seats—the front row with only a railing to separate them from the arena dirt.

He pressed his hand to the small of her back and guided her past the back row. "You've got front row seats. Nothing but the best."

Sydney sat in one of the chairs he indicated, between Jace and Lacey. She glanced over at the chutes and the catwalk behind them, where several nervous-looking cowboys stood. Her pulse ramped up as the electrically charged air seemed to permeate her. Not unlike the tenseness she'd experienced before competing in a dressage event—something the fans never felt in their seats. Even Jace was apparently affected, despite all his experience, as he was seemingly unaware of his right leg jiggling up and down. She bit down on the smile threatening to emerge. She wanted to share the similarity with him, but fear held her back. Fear that she may cross the point of no return with him, and then it would be too late.

"Hey, Sydney, I need to ready Shiloh for the parade. I'll be back to sit with you as soon as I can."

Syd nodded and Lacy scurried over to the stairs.

Jace shifted in the seat next to her and pointed at her feet. "I just noticed. You're wearing different boots. You didn't buy some, did you?"

She almost burst out laughing at his grin. He really was enjoying her dressing the part. "My girlfriend Erin loaned these to me, along with the shirt and the jeans. She didn't want me to be out of place. I have Lacy's boots in the car."

"The same gal who watches the NFR?"

"Yes. I had no idea she liked rodeo so much until I mentioned I was coming here."

"You don't have your own jeans?"

"Of course I do, but according to Erin, my stylish skinny jeans aren't right for a rodeo because the jeans should be worn over the boots, not tucked inside them."

He laughed. "They would have been okay. Maybe she should have come with you."

"Erin may love rodeo, but she loves her fiancé more. She wouldn't go anywhere like this without him. They're busy planning their wedding." She glanced around. "I hope you didn't have to pull strings to get these seats."

He shrugged. "So I called in a chip or two. I've competed here long enough to get some perks."

"Do you know when you'll be riding for your event?"

"I'm going first. I'll have to leave at intermission."

"What do you do to prepare?"

"I put on my chaps, my spurs, and my vest, and then I pray a lot."

"Vest?"

"It's protection in case a bull steps on my chest or tries to gore me there."

She grimaced at the dangerous reminder. At least he wore some protection. "You told that cowboy earlier you'd tried to use a helmet but stopped after only one time. Don't you want to get used to a helmet if it would protect you? You already wear a vest."

"A helmet blocks my peripheral vision. The guys coming up in the ranks are used to them because now they're mandatory in high-school rodeo. I never had to wear one. Like I told Tyler earlier, I leave it to God."

She held back the comment poised on her tongue. If she said she always wore a helmet while competing in dressage and it wasn't a distraction, she'd start a discussion she didn't want to have. Sydney rubbed her hands over her jeans. Jace left his safety to God, and she needed to do the same.

He reached over and squeezed her hand. "Don't worry about me, Syd. Bull riding is risky, but I hold the sport in deep respect and I'm as careful as possible. I've been doing this for about half my life, and the worst that's happened is a broken leg during a college rodeo. There are good medical people around, and the Lord's protected me so far. I trust He'll continue until I retire."

She relaxed under his grip and he let go. "How long do bull riders ride before they retire?"

"Some end their careers early, and others go into their thirties. I'm hoping to last to my midthirties. Another five years or so and my ranch and stock-contracting business should be in good shape."

"If you still have the ranch."

He fastened a flinty gaze on her as his jaw muscle popped against his cheek. "I'm not as foolhardy as you think. Trust me, I'm not losing the ranch. Period. My tax lawyer is working with the IRS." He took a folded paper from his shirt pocket and shook it open before studying what looked to be a list.

Finally, a reaction to the seriousness of his situation she could believe. But his answer still left her unsettled. His lawyer could likely work out a payback plan on installments, but why dig the hole deeper by paying a huge fine to Frisky's? Her job still wasn't done.

"McGowan, we need to talk." A stocky-looking man wearing the usual cowboy uniform of jeans, boots, and a Stetson stood below the railing with a clipboard in hand.

Jace climbed over the rail and dropped to the ground. The man pointed at something on the clipboard and Jace frowned. After more discussion, Jace nodded and said what looked like "Okay."

He returned to his seat the same way he came, his expression solemn. "The bull I drew took sick. The vet pulled him. I had a choice between two others."

He slumped in his seat and scowled.

"Are the other bulls harder to ride?"

He shook his head. "No. They're easier."

Syd relaxed and mentally thanked God.

"I liked my draw. He was the rankest one in tonight's pen. The only other animal ranker is my own bull, and I can't ride him. But sometimes even a docile bull can fool a person. Hopefully, this will be one of those nights. I need that prize money."

"Are you still the first to go?"

"No, now I'm third. I prefer to go last, because that way I know what I need to do to win."

She thought through their previous conversations. "You mean you need to win the money to qualify for the tournament in December, right?"

"Yeah, but we don't call it a tournament. It's the Finals. Only the top money winners throughout the season qualify to go."

"What if you don't qualify?"

He worked his pursed lips back and forth several times. "Then I have to live with it and find another way to get some extra dough."

"Seems to me you'd better plan on renegotiating with Frisky's whether I ride the horse tomorrow or—"

The announcer's voice interrupted the country music, saying they were one song away from the start of the rodeo.

She glanced at Jace. He'd sunk lower into his seat and crossed his arms over his chest. Maybe he was rethinking his ride. He'd told her earlier how he liked to study the bull's usual way of jumping and turning, visualizing the ride before it happened.

They sat in silence until the music stopped. A man with a microphone in his hand galloped into the center of the arena on a chestnut quarter horse. He welcomed the crowd. Then cowgirls, with their blinged-out shirts sparkling in the overhead lights, galloped their horses into the arena. The flags they carried unfurled over their heads.

"Those are the queens."

Syd stared at Jace. "I hope you don't call them that to their faces."

"They don't care. That's what we all call them. There's Miss Teen Rodeo Illinois and Miss Rodeo Illinois, and the lady with the American Flag is Miss Rodeo America. Nothing disrespectful intended."

"I have a lot to learn."

"Sounds like you intend to not make this your first and only rodeo." He nudged her with his elbow and flashed an adorable grin.

"I didn't mean that."

"Could have fooled me."

Sydney's stomach knotted. But for a few critical moments in her past, she could still be feeling the wind in her hair as her horse powered its way across a stretch of trail. Maybe after tomorrow...

She shook her head and brought her focus back to the arena. The queen carrying the American flag brought her horse to the center of the arena while the other women stopped their horses on either side of her.

After everyone stood for the Star-Spangled Banner and a prayer, men and women on horseback filed into the arena. The numbers affixed to their backs flapped in the breeze. Sydney spotted Lacy on the far side of the dirt and kept her eyes on the blond barrel racer until she passed by the VIP section. She returned Lacy's wave before facing Jace. "Would you have been riding Charley in the parade if I wasn't here?"

"Not tonight. I'm not competing in calf roping until tomorrow night. I'll ride then. Don't need a horse to bull-ride."

Sydney listened intently as Jace kept a running commentary through what he called the timed events. So consumed with watching calves being roped and steers wrestled to the ground, she didn't notice when Lacy returned.

Sydney wanted to hate the rodeo, but she loved every part of it—especially how well-trained the horses were for the roping events. It would be easy to adapt to this lifestyle, and that made her dread her imminent parting from Jace even more.

Lacy leaned slightly over Sydney. "Hey, cuz, if you want to get down to the chutes early, I can sit here through the rest of the steer wrestling."

"Thanks, but I'm good."

Lacy glanced at Sydney. "How are you liking the rodeo so far?"

"It's nice."

Lacy shrugged. " 'Nice' is better than hating it."

"I think she doesn't want to admit that she likes it. I saw a hint of a smile on her face a few times." Jace's elbow poked her.

She elbowed him back. "I was smiling at the clown, not the competition."

"Or maybe a hunky cowboy or two." Lacy laughed and winked at Sydney.

Sydney resisted the temptation to check how Jace reacted to the comment.

The crowd burst out laughing at the clown. Disappointed that she'd missed what the man wearing baggy pants and a floppy hat had said to the announcer, she caught Jace's eye and asked what was so funny.

"I was busy listening to the two of you and didn't catch it." He took her hand for the second time. "You enjoying all this?"

She nodded. "Oh, yes."

He squeezed her hand. "Good." This time he didn't let go right away, and for once, she was glad he didn't.

At intermission, Lacy left to get her horse ready for the barrel racing, and a few minutes later Jace stood. "Time for me to make my exit. Bull riding is up right after the barrel racing. I'll meet you here after my ride."

She met his gaze with her own and asked, "What do people say to a bull rider before he rides?"

" 'Ride for eight' is good."

"Ride for eight." She held up her hand and they high-fived. Then he closed his hand over her fingers and squeezed. "Thanks. See ya on the flip side." He stepped to the catwalk behind the chutes and disappeared down some steps as she mentally offered up a prayer for his safety.

13

Jace grabbed his bull rope that he'd already heated up with rosin. Major Damage, his newly assigned bull, waited in the runway to be let into the bucking chutes. He stepped up on the metal rail next to the bull. Someone had already draped the flank strap over the animal's backside.

"I heard your first draw got pulled." Clint came up beside him. "Tough luck."

Jace tossed his bull rope over the bull. The animal barely shivered. This wasn't the bovine's first outing. He knew what to expect. "I think whoever named this dude 'Major Damage' had some magical thinking going on. From what I've heard about him, he's not very damaging."

Clint shrugged. "Don't be so sure. I saw him buck up in Wisconsin last weekend, and he tossed a good hand in two seconds. He jumps high coming out of the gate and then usually turns right before going back left. Not Bushwacker by any stretch, but he could cause major damage if you're not careful. Pun intended."

"Thanks for the rundown. Good to know."

A few feet away, the barrel racers lined up for their event. Jace spotted Lacy and sent her a thumbs-up. She tipped her hat along with her usual grin.

The barrel racing began, and after the first horse and rider galloped into the arena, the bulls began loading into the chutes. Jace's bull went into the Crawford Memorial Hospital chute, and he chuckled to himself. *I hope this isn't a sign that I'll end up spending the night there.* He banished the thought as fast as it appeared. Negative thinking before a ride was never good.

The announcer gave the stats on the final barrel racer and declared Lacy the winner. Jace allowed himself a quick smile, then pushed the rest of the announcer's words into the background. The first rider bucked off at 7.1 seconds. Jace offered up a quick prayer for focus and protection, then stood by the chute and waited while the second rider stayed on for eighty-two points. Jace handed the end of his bull rope to another rider to pull before climbing over the chute rail and resting his feet on the rails on either side of the bull. He pressed his foot on the animal's back to let him know a rider was about to get on. Satisfied the beast wouldn't startle, he eased down onto the animal, keeping his feet on the side rails and taking care to not let his spurs touch the bull.

His pulse amped up and an empty feeling filled the pit of his stomach. What had Clint said? He visualized how he would counter the right turn the bull usually made and prepare for the next turn to the left.

Jace grabbed the rope from the puller, then ran his gloved hand up and down over the rosin-covered area until the goo heated and felt sticky. He inserted his hand in the rope handle, wrapped the rope's tail around his hand, and tossed the remaining length over the beast's hump. After positioning his body, he pressed his legs against the bull's sides, then tucked his chin and gave the gate guy a nod.

The chute opened, and the bull propelled into the arena with a high jump to the left. Jace moved all his weight toward the inside of the turn and leaned his shoulders the direction of the spin. The bull jumped again and switched directions. Jace shoved back with his hips and lifted on the rope.

On the next jump, the bull changed direction again and Jace quickly crossed his free arm in front of his body. In his fist, the rope slipped. He had to keep his grip, not look away. The rope slipped again. Finally, the horn blew and Jace released the rope and leaped off. His boot landed on something hard before his face hit the dirt.

He spit clay out of his mouth and glanced around. Where was that rascal? Clint and the other bullfighter's shouts were off to his left. Jace scrambled onto his knees as his gaze jerked from one side of the arena to the other.

"Jace, head to the chutes. You're clear."

At Clint's command, he crawled across the dirt and into the chute he'd just exited. Someone slammed the gate. He turned and peered through the slats. Major Damage sauntered along the arena's far side past the timed-event chutes. A pickup cowboy chased after him with a rope. Jace scanned for Clint and the other bullfighter. If either of those guys got hurt on his account... His gaze found the men off to the side, and relief rushed over him.

Jace looked up at the inky sky, starless because of the overhead lights, and thanked God for His protection. He then stole a glance into the VIP section. Lacy's thumbs-up was great, but seeing Sydney's grin lifted his spirits more than the applause.

"Eighty-eight points!" the announcer shouted into his microphone. "We have a new leader, folks. Jace McGowan survived what could have been a terrible ending to a great ride." The crowd cheered.

By now the bull had been herded back to the pen. Jace stepped out into the arena and waved his hat as Clint came up and handed him his bull rope. "Great ride, McGowan."

Jace thanked him and strode to the gate, with the bell attached to the rope clanging as it hit his leg with each step. He noticed the usual adrenaline rush that followed a good ride fading faster than usual. All that mattered now was Syd's cheering him on.

They were already waiting for the next rider to take his turn, but Sydney's adrenaline had to be pulsing through her body at warp speed. Her pulse hadn't slowed since Jace waved his acknowledgment of the crowd's cheers. She looked at Lacy. "Will Jace join us now that his ride is done?"

"Probably not. The rodeo is almost over. If he's the top rider of the night, they'll want him to step out onto the dirt for an encore."

"Then I guess I'll wait here for him. I had no idea how exciting rodeos were."

Lacy's eyes sparkled. "Only two more riders to go. Jace looks to have this one in the bag. He has a good chance at the overall too."

"So you're hoping the next guys buck off, huh?"

Lacy laughed. "I don't care if they ride, just so they don't score as high as Jace. Besides, the next bull is one of Jace's, and we want a high bull score. I'm hoping the rider bucks off—without injuries, of course."

Sydney cast a sideways glance at Lacy. "I'm glad to hear you say 'without injuries.'"

Lacy's expression dissolved and she laid a hand on Sydney's arm. "Oh, Syd, I guess I'm so used to how things work in rodeo that I do sound matter-of-fact about things. I'm always anxious about safety—for Clint and the other bullfighters too. It's all part of bull riding. The bullfighters take as many chances as the riders—sometimes even more. They don't get enough credit, as far as I'm concerned. You saw how Clint got the bull's attention off Jace and had to make some quick moves not to get hurt himself."

Sydney nodded. "I did notice that. I'd hate to see how the whole thing would have ended without Clint putting himself between the bull and Jace."

The next bull ride involved Jace's bull, Oreo. The rider bucked off at seven seconds. According to Lacy's play-by-play, the bull received a very high score while the rider got nothing. Only one ride to go and Jace could be declared the winner of the night's competition.

From her seat, Sydney searched behind the chutes for Jace and spotted him leaning against a railing while talking with another cowboy. The rider in the chute was taking longer than the other riders had. Out on the arena floor, the clown kibitzed with the announcer, telling him how he'd shopped the local garage sales that day.

"Ladies and gentlemen, this is our last bull ride for the night. If the score isn't higher than Jace McGowan's eighty-eight, then Jace is tonight's winner and the man to beat for the overall."

The chute opened, and the bull soared into the arena as if airborne.

"Whoa!" Lacy shouted. "This ride could beat Jace's if the guy doesn't buck off."

The bull spun one way a couple times and then switched directions and jumped. The rider leaned back, his free arm going behind his head. As the bull came down on his front feet, the rider jerked forward and flew into the air. He landed inches away from the animal, who continued bucking, his backside rising high in the air.

The cowboy lay motionless, and Sydney whispered a prayer for his protection.

To distract the bull, the bullfighters, off to the side of the fallen cowboy, shouted and waved their arms at the animal. The bull pawed the ground, holding his stare on the rider. Clint moved closer to the bull and shouted the animal's name. The bull turned, bowed his head, and charged Clint. The bullfighter jumped to his right, but the bull's head barreled into Clint's chest. He quickly raised his snout, and Clint catapulted into the air before dropping to the ground like a rag doll, his motionless body several feet away from the rider's.

"Clint's out cold." Lacy jumped to her feet and shouted, "Come on, Clint. Wake up!"

Sydney's silent prayers for the men barraged heaven as a hush fell over the arena.

Jace and several other cowboys scrambled over the chute railings and ran to the downed men. Across the arena, a cowboy on horseback roped the bull and the other bullfighter raced to Clint's side.

Uniformed paramedics jogged into the arena next, with two of them carrying backboards. One came up beside Jace, who was kneeling next to his friend. He gently tugged Jace to his feet as a couple of other first responders squatted beside Clint and began assessing him. Jace seemed to hesitate, but after a few moments, he stepped back.

Sydney glanced at Lacy, who was sitting again. Her lips moved without sound in what looked to be a repeated prayer. Sydney joined her by saying out loud, "Please, Lord, let these men live."

Moments that felt like hours passed before the cowboy sat up. A couple of bull riders helped him to his feet while another picked up his discarded helmet. The crowd applauded as he gave a weak wave and looked toward the VIP section.

Sydney gasped. "Lacy, is that the guy Jace talked to before we came to our seats?"

"Sure looks like him. Praise God, he looks to be okay."

Sydney turned her focus to Clint and strained to see a rise in his chest. If there was one, it was so slight she couldn't see it.

An ambulance drove through the gate and halted a few feet from Clint.

Lacy grabbed Sydney's hand. "Let's pray." She bowed her head. "Father, You are not surprised by this, and You have Clint in Your grasp. We pray for him to wake up and recover."

At Lacy's amen, Sydney opened her eyes and released her grip on Lacy's hand. "Sorry if I cut off your blood flow."

"Hey, I was holding on as tightly as you." Lacy glanced toward the arena. "Here comes Jace."

He ran up to the railing. "Sydney, they're taking Clint to the hospital in Robinson. They won't let me ride in the ambulance. Can you drive me there?"

Warning beeps sounded, and Sydney looked over Jace's head. The ambulance was backing up toward the open gate. She looked again at Jace. His eyes were full of anxiety. "I'll meet you by my car."

Jace nodded and jogged toward the gate.

Sydney picked up her purse. "Lacy, are you coming with us?"

Lacy shook her head. "I think it's best if I stay here. Too many people crowding the hospital isn't good. I'll make sure Jace's bulls are back in the pen. Call me when you know something. Jace has my number."

The announcer assured the people that Clint would have the best of care, and with that, the bull ride and the rodeo were over.

Sydney scurried toward the steps. The ambulance siren wailed as it headed down the lane, the sound diminishing as it advanced toward the road. She met Jace at her car. He tossed his duffel into the backseat and climbed in. "We need to get out before the parking lot becomes a logjam."

The ambulance had already cleared the parked cars and was turning onto the road by the time Sydney and Jace started up the lane. They made it halfway to the exit before cars started to stream onto the pavement ahead of them. Sydney hit the brakes. "Sorry I didn't make it out in time."

"Not your fault." Jace rubbed the back of his neck. "I wish this line would move. We're just sitting here."

She had to stay composed to keep him calm. "You and Clint are really close, aren't you?"

"Yeah, he's like my brother."

"Did they say what his injuries are?"

"The bull's horn likely punctured a lung. He was bleeding from his chest. His left leg is broken too. Part of the bone was sticking out."

A sour taste rose in Sydney's mouth, and she swallowed it along with words that would ask him to stop being so descriptive. He didn't need to be stifled as much as encouraged to talk. "Don't bullfighters wear vests like bull riders?"

"A different type that isn't as bulky, yes. They aren't 100-percent puncture-proof. The bull's horn likely broke through a seam. The animal came at him from an angle."

The traffic crept toward the exit, and a few minutes later, her car broke free of the grounds and followed a line of red taillights snaking through darkened streets toward the highway. A sense of intimacy settled over Sydney and Jace during the silent ride—one of those times when words weren't necessary in the company of a good friend. At the edge of town, Sydney sped up with the other cars, but they were still barely going the posted speed limit. Red lights on the truck ahead of them flashed, and she braked quickly.

Jace groaned. "There are never this many cars at the stop sign."

"You probably never drive this way so soon after the rodeo." Sydney eased the vehicle forward. "Only a couple more cars to go."

Once in town, they followed blue-and-white hospital signs until they came to the one-story facility. Jace let out an acerbic chuckle. "I bucked out of the hospital's chute tonight and hoped it wasn't a sign I'd end up here. Never thought Clint would."

Sydney pulled under a large portico that protected the emergency-room entrance and stopped. Jace opened his door and jumped out the moment she released the locks. "See you inside."

She found a parking spot, then ran across the blacktop toward the ER. The glass doors slid open, and she stepped into a moderately sized waiting area. A medicinal smell assaulted her senses, and she had to work to not let her mind dig up memories best buried. Across the room, Jace stood at a counter, along with a young woman holding a baby.

Sydney drew in a breath and came up next to him as the grandmotherly woman behind the counter offered him a sympathetic expression. "I'm sorry, Mr. McGowan. I can't let you go back there while they're working on your friend. He's in good hands. I'll make sure the doctor finds you and gives you an update as soon as there is one."

Jace's jaw pulsed as he appeared to think over the woman's words. He leaned an elbow on the counter and looked directly at her. "I'm like family to him. We're not from around here. I promise I'll stand back and not get in the way."

The woman puffed her cheeks, then blew out a breath. She was soon going to lose her patience.

Sydney rested her hand on Jace's arm. "She's right, Jace. They need to work on him without worrying about nonmedical people being in the way. Let's sit over there." She indicated some chairs a short distance away.

He raised his hands and stepped back, addressing the woman. "As soon as they say it's okay, find me."

"Most assuredly, sir."

Sydney followed as Jace stalked across the waiting area toward the chairs she suggested. He yanked off his Stetson and sat in a chair. He set the hat on the empty seat to his left, then rested his elbows on his knees and buried his face in his hands.

Sydney slid into the seat to his right.

Jace's throbbing jaw muscle finally slowed. He raised his head and looked at her. "Thanks for staying."

"No need to thank me. I know what it's like to be alone in a hospital, waiting for word on a loved one."

"Are you talking about your dad's accident?"

"Yes."

"I should have asked her to send word to Clint that I'm out here so he knows he's not alone."

"He must know you wouldn't disregard this."

Jace shrugged and rubbed his eyes with the heels of his hands. "I suppose so. This isn't the first time one of us has been hurt, and we've always been there for each other. But this injury is much worse than any we've had."

Sydney swallowed against the growing lump in her throat. She longed to wrap her arms around him and tell him that everything would be okay, but she didn't know if that was the truth. "How long have you and Clint been friends?"

"Since high school. We were on the rodeo team together. After graduation, I went on to college and he stayed behind, bucking in the rodeo circuit for a year. Then he decided to switch to bullfighting. His dad deserted him and his mom when he was a kid. After I started working full time at the ranch, I convinced my dad to hire him. He moved into the bunkhouse and has been there ever since."

"Maybe his mom should know what happened tonight."

He shrugged. "I doubt she cares. She's a drinker."

"She's still his mother. I'd give her the chance to make that decision."

"You're right. I've been telling myself it isn't serious enough to call." He pulled his cell phone from his pocket, then stuffed it back in. "Best to wait until I have something concrete to say."

"Good idea."

He twisted in his seat and faced Sydney. "This is going to be a long night. If you want to go on to the hotel, I'll be okay."

Sydney glanced at her watch. Had they only been there fifteen minutes? "I'm not going anywhere. I want to know how Clint is too. Besides, how would you get back to the arena?"

He slumped into his seat and stretched out his legs. "I can always call when I'm ready."

"Nice try, but you're stuck with me."

He grabbed her hand and squeezed it. "Let's clear up one thing. I never feel stuck with you."

His words warmed her, but she didn't respond. It was best to say nothing at all.

He opened his mouth as if he were going to speak, but he shut it when a doctor in blue scrubs approached them.

"Are you Jace McGowan?"

Jace let go of Sydney's hand and stood. "Yes, sir."

"I'm Dr. Cassidy. I've been told you're Mr. Palmer's next of kin."

Jace stared at his feet a second, then looked up. "The only family he's got around here."

The doctor nodded and looked at Sydney. "Are you with Mr. McGowan?"

"Yes, but I'm not—"

"I'm fine with your coming with us. Let's go over there where we can talk." The doctor indicated an unoccupied part of the waiting area away from the admitting desk.

Sydney gathered her purse while her throat ached from holding back a sob. "You go ahead, Jace. Call me if you need a ride back to the arena."

"Come on, Sydney. Don't leave yet." His hoarse whisper was more a plea than a command.

Impatience shone in the doctor's eyes. This wasn't a battle that needed fighting.

"Okay." Sydney followed behind Jace and Dr. Cassidy to an arrangement of three chairs. The doctor gathered empty paper cups stuffed with crumpled napkins from the table situated in front of the chairs, tossing the mess in a nearby trash can. He sat and waited for Sydney and Jace to sit across from him.

Dr. Cassidy moved to the edge of his seat and looked Jace in the eyes. "Clint is a lucky man. The horn made a rather large puncture wound through the chest wall and into his left lung. We tried to treat it by using tubes and going down through his throat, but the wound is too large. It needs to be closed ASAP. He's on his way to surgery right now."

Jace folded his hands in his lap and studied them. He looked up at the doctor. "No offense, but wouldn't it be better to transfer Clint to a larger hospital?"

The doctor's face showed no signs of being insulted. "We may be small, but we're fortunate to have Dr. Edington on staff here. He's as good a surgeon as they come. Moving Clint to Champaign or Indianapolis would be risky."

Jace swallowed hard and nodded. "How long will the surgery take?"

"Hard to say until the surgeon gets in there. Two hours, maybe longer. Clint also has a break in his left fibula. That's the large bone in the lower leg. They'll set it while he's under."

Jace's expression remained grave. "What's the prognosis?"

"There's always a chance of things going wrong, but I anticipate that he'll be okay after a long winter of healing. Where does he live?"

"On my ranch outside San Antonio. He's a ranch hand and helps with my bull stock business."

"He'll need to check in with a pulmonary specialist and an orthopedist there." The doctor stood and looked from Jace to Sydney. "You two can wait in the surgical waiting room." He gave them instructions on how to find it and left.

They stood, and Jace started toward the door the doctor had indicated. When Sydney didn't follow, he stopped and faced her. "You coming?"

A voice inside her seemed to shout, *"Leave now! Don't let down your guard."* If she were smart, she'd listen to the voice the way she had ever since that terrible day when Ryan announced he was leaving her. But this time Jace's needs trumped hers. Waiting alone while a loved one underwent emergency surgery wasn't easy. She'd have to take a risk and stay.

14

Dark blue upholstered chairs and a sofa, all with wood trim, filled the small surgical waiting area. A clock on the far wall above a pair of vending machines showed 12:10 a.m. Sydney walked to the only window, poked her fingers between the blinds, and peeked out. In the parking lot, her Prius sat under an overhead mercury light—one of the two vehicles in the lot.

She'd experienced a roller coaster of emotions since arriving at the arena—apprehension, excitement, regret, fear, sadness, and now worry. The Bible cautioned her not to worry about tomorrow because today had enough trouble of its own. Another verse said to be anxious for nothing and give everything to God; His peace would take over. But she wasn't worried about tomorrow right then. What about the next hour or two while Clint was in surgery?

Please, Lord, grant Clint Your strength to get through this surgery and heal.

Sydney turned. Jace sat slumped against the sofa back, his arms folded and his Stetson placed over his face. He'd removed his boots and propped his stocking feet on the coffee table, and his chest rose and fell with each steady breath. She'd been at the window longer than she thought.

Jace repositioned his legs, crossing his feet at the ankles, but he didn't wake up. A warm feeling washed over her, and her breath hitched as she realized that she didn't ever want to say good-bye to this man again. But that meant she had to trust him. Seeing how committed and faithful he was to Clint should have been enough. But a bond of friendship between two men was different. He claimed that his reputation as a player wasn't true, and she wanted to believe him. If only that nagging voice in her head would stop telling her to *not* believe him, that he was no different than the others.

Careful to keep her boot heels from clomping on the floor, Sydney crossed to a chair placed at a right angle to the couch. She toed off her boots and curled her feet under her. If she turned on the flat-screen TV, she'd take the chance of waking him. Instead, she selected a five-month-old *People Magazine* from a stack on an end table, flipping past the usual gossip until an article about the new lead in the next season of *The Bachelor* jumped out at her. A twenty-something man smiled from his promotion photo. Good-looking, but Jace had him beat by a mile.

"You don't have to sit over there."

She started and looked up.

Blue eyes much deeper and more inviting than the ones in the magazine met hers.

"I assumed you were napping."

"Praying. No way could I sleep."

Sydney tossed the magazine aside and moved to the cushion beside him. "I thought maybe this kind of thing is routine for you."

He draped his arm loosely over her shoulders. "*This* never becomes routine. But God's got it, and I trust Clint will pull through." He dug into his jeans pocket and pulled out a handful of coins. "I'm sure the coffee in that machine doesn't hold a candle to your favorite coffee shop, but do you want some? I've gotta have a jolt of caffeine, no matter how awful it tastes."

Sydney yawned. As much as she detested vending-machine coffee, a cup of strong java sounded good. "Thanks. Make mine with extra cream and sugar."

"You don't usually take sugar, do you?"

"Anything to mask the taste."

"Coffee with the works for the lady." He picked up his hat and plopped it onto Sydney's head before he stood. "It looks better on you."

Sydney pushed it out of her eyes. "It may if it were several sizes smaller." She removed the hat and the motion sent Jace's familiar aroma of cowboy and outdoors through the air. If he could bottle it, she'd buy a dozen.

Coins clinked into the machine, jolting her back to reality. Jace bent to retrieve a steaming cup from the cubicle, seemingly unaware that she was appreciating the way he filled out his jeans. His daily runs likely contributed to that, but being a hands-on rancher probably worked his muscles in ways running didn't. She leaned her head against the couch cushion and shut her eyes, pushing away thoughts of how she could do life with Jace and still keep her career goals intact. She was crazy to even think those thoughts when she had no reason to.

"Drink at your own risk."

Sydney's eyes popped open as Jace set a steaming paper cup on the coffee table. He padded back to the machine and dropped more coins into the slot.

She lifted the foamy brew, then took a sip. The tasteless liquid seared its way into her stomach. She set the drink on the table in front of her and waved her hand in front of her mouth. "Warning: the stuff is lethally hot. I may need a doctor for second-degree burns to my throat."

Jace returned to the sofa and set his coffee on the end table. "That bad?"

"I think blisters are forming on my tongue."

He sat and then gripped her chin between his thumb and index finger, nudging her mouth open. "Let me have a look." He peered into her mouth. "No blisters yet."

His gaze fell to her parted lips, and she tensed. She wanted to feel his lips on hers one more time, but kissing would only make the impending parting hurt more. "Good to hear." She turned and picked up her coffee, causing his hand to drop away.

Jace shifted and grabbed the television remote, aiming it at the monitor ... but he didn't push the POWER button. Still holding the device, he ran his gaze over her face until their eyes met. She wanted to look away, but the magnetic pull of his stare was stronger than her will. He blinked and tossed the remote onto the table. "Sydney Knight, you're way too kissable, and it makes me crazy."

She stared at her lap. "Yeah. I feel the same about you."

"So what are we going to do about it?"

The answer she wanted to say wasn't the right one. She picked up the remote and pressed the POWER button. An old *I Love Lucy* show filled the screen. "Watch TV?"

He took the remote in hand and hit the OFF button. "Not so fast, Syd. It's time to have a talk."

A sinking feeling came over her. "What's to talk about?" She gripped the end of the remote she still held and pulled at it.

He covered her hand with his. "That we both enjoy kissing each other is a start. Then we can move on to how we feel about each other apart from kissing. No more games."

"I wasn't playing games."

"I didn't say *you* were. You first." He squeezed her hand.

"No fair. You're the one who started this conversation. Besides, why bother discussing it when in a couple days we'll go our separate ways? I already explained why any kind of relationship between us wouldn't work. In fact, I'm hoping to leave tomorrow after the challenge."

"Not good enough. There's more you aren't saying. But I guess you're not ready." Jace took the remote from her hand and pressed a button. The screen came to life, and he scrolled through the channels, past infomercials, a *Brady Bunch* rerun, and a talk show.

Sydney's eyes closed and she leaned her head back. It was just as well he'd turned on the television.

"Now we're talkin'."

Her eyes opened as a bull bucked off a cowboy on the screen. "Bull riding is on TV? Who knew?"

"The PBR is on at least once a week during the season, and they repeat the events overnight."

"Is bull riding all you think about?"

"Not hardly. There's God, the ranch, my family, and lately..." He slipped his arm around her waist and tugged her closer. "You."

The warm, fuzzy feeling returned to her stomach.

He gently nudged her head until it rested on his shoulder. "You know, Syd, I'm crazy about you. There must be some way for us to be able to breathe the same air and not stay apart. To give ourselves a chance to see whether this thing between us is sustainable. I'd be willing to come to Illinois if I can make a few adjustments."

Surely he wasn't serious. She wriggled out of his embrace and stared at him. "How can you run the ranch from Illinois? What about your bull business? The twins. Your mom."

Hurt-filled eyes stared back at her. "See? I was right. It is more than you needing to stay in Chicago because of work."

She slid to the other end of the couch. If she told him the real reason, he'd never understand. How could he, when he was willing to take a risk every time he got on a bull? "You'll have to trust me on this."

He inched his way over the cushions until he was beside her. "If Clint is going to be hospitalized for a while, I can't leave on Sunday. I know it's asking a lot because of your set time with your mom, but I don't suppose you can stay an extra day?" He slid his arm across her shoulders and tugged her closer. "Maybe with more time we can work out a solution."

Sydney didn't move. "My mother will be hurt if I'm not with her on Labor Day. It's a tradition."

"The anniversary of your dad's accident. Tell me about him."

Keep your voice uplifted. You know the drill. "What do you want to know?"

"I have a sense there's more to your dad's death than you let on. What is it?"

It was tempting to say as little as possible, like she usually did when asked, but Jace was different. It was time to let down one of her walls. "He was riding back to me because I'd been thrown by my horse after he was spooked by a snake. His horse saw the same snake and reared up. My dad flew off and hit his head on a rock. He was conscious for only a minute or so. I wasn't hurt at all, but he didn't know that until I got to him just before he passed. He said he hoped he had set a good example for me to follow."

Tears trailed down her cheeks, and Sydney palmed them away. She looked off to the side.

Jace pulled her closer and gently pressed her head against his chest. A minute or two passed in silence. She sniffed and she felt him lean forward, then nudge her with something harder than his hand.

She opened her eyes. He'd grabbed the tissue box from the table in front of them. "Thanks." She sat up and plucked a couple of tissues from the box and blew her nose. With another tissue, she dabbed at the skin under her eyes, certain she bore a strong resemblance to a raccoon.

Jace rested his bent finger under her chin and turned her head until their gazes locked. Moisture glinted in his eyes. "Thanks for telling me. I can see how difficult it was to relive it."

"So do you understand now why I feel so strongly about the legal clinic he founded? He asked me to follow his example, and that's what I am doing."

"I wish I could have met your father. He sounds like a wonderful man. But, Syd, what if by following his example, he meant more to a strong faith in God and good character and morals, not what God called him to do?"

Her gaze surveyed the room—the vending machine, the clock, a tear in one of the chair cushions... She fought the urge to go to the disarrayed pile of magazines and stack them neatly. She looked at Jace. "It was more than taking his words at face value. For a long time, I felt responsible for Dad's death, and carrying out his dream was a way to make it up to him."

Jace searched her face with his eyes. "Oh, Syd, you couldn't help what happened with your horse getting spooked. Your dad did what any father would have done in racing back to you."

"I realize that now, but back then I couldn't shake the thought that if my horse hadn't spooked, my dad would not have died. I finally overcame the feeling thanks to prayer and counseling."

"Why didn't you regroup after you realized you weren't at fault?"

"Two years in law school meant lots of tuition money and hours of study, and I found I really did enjoy a lot about the law. Harry had assured me of a position in the firm and was mentoring me. It was as if I was given Dad's job, in a way. It wasn't just guilt for my dad's death I had to overcome, but guilt for my brother's accident too."

She clamped her mouth shut. It was one thing to let down a wall, but two walls were too much. He'd think her an emotional mess for sure. Besides, he was the one who was supposed to be comforted in his angst about Clint.

Jace began kneading her neck. "You're really tense, Syd. If you don't want to talk about it, I'm cool with it."

The tenderness in his voice seemed to push away the last of her uneasiness. "Thanks. I'm okay. I was mad at my brother for teasing me the morning of that last game—the one where he got hurt—so I'd hid the 'lucky' socks he always wore. When he couldn't find them, he accused me of taking them, saying that I'd broken his concentration and he'd probably mess up in the game. That all came roaring back to me when Dad died. Usually a man wants to see his son take his place in the world, but Nate's accident changed that idea. By filling my dad's empty shoes, I was able to assuage both guilts."

"What had you wanted to do before you decided to be a lawyer?"

She inched out of the cocoon of his arm. "It doesn't matter. I'm a lawyer now, and I really do like the work. Guilt made me choose my profession, but the good side is, I'll be helping others to turn their lives around and make better choices once I'm in the courtroom."

An awkward silence fell between them. Sydney reached for her purse and pulled out her cell phone. The screen display told her what she already knew: no reception. She dropped the instrument into her bag, thankful that Jace had apparently let the subject drop.

Jace sipped his coffee, made a face, and set it on the coffee table. "Time for a lighter subject. My family came to Chicago a couple of times when I was a kid and my grandparents were still alive. My mom told me the other day that you and I played together."

She grinned at him, noticing how his overnight stubble had merged with his permanent five-o'clock shadow. "You're kidding. Really?"

His eyes twinkled. "Really. Isn't that crazy? She said Uncle Harry always held a barbeque when we were in town, and his law partner—your dad—was there with his family. She remembers a pretty, blond-haired girl they called Syddie."

She hadn't heard anyone say her old nickname since she'd started first grade and announced that she was going to be "Sydney" from then on. "Wow. Who knew? Don't take it personally, but I don't remember you at all."

He laughed. "Nor do I remember you. To think we were playmates on occasion, never dreaming that, years later, we'd be in each other's company again. And I'm so glad we are." He moved a curl from her face, his fingertips feathering her cheek.

Tingles ran down her neck and back. She couldn't move if she'd wanted to. And she didn't want to.

"It's kinda cool to think we met back then. That would make this thing between us not so whirlwind after all. We've known each other for decades, in a way." He leaned in and drew her into a tender, lingering kiss.

His beard rubbed against her cheek, feeling surprisingly soft. She cupped her hand around his neck and drew him closer. A soft sigh came from his throat. Maybe she *could* stay until Monday.

The kiss broke and he rested his forehead on hers. "The six-year-old me had no idea what the little blond-haired girl named Syddie had in store for me in the future. I wonder what I would have done if I'd known." He kissed the tip of her nose and sat back a bit.

"At that age, you probably would have thought, 'Ewwww.' "

"True, but I'm sure you were the cutest little girl there."

She giggled. "I hate to burst your bubble, but I was gangly with braces and glasses as thick as those soda-pop bottles people used to drink from."

He laughed and took her hand, weaving their fingers together. "Glasses?"

"Contacts are the best invention ever."

"I wasn't much of a looker, either. Short and pudgy."

"You? Pudgy?"

"Yeah, I had to grow a foot before I caught up to my weight." Still holding her hand, he ran his index finger down her cheek in a light, gentle stroke. "I like having you wait with me, but if you want to go back to the hotel, I understand."

She squeezed his hand. "And let you sit here alone, not knowing what's going on with Clint? I'm not going anywhere."

"Good answer." He drew her back into the cozy spot under his arm. "You've had a lot of heartache and difficulties."

She snuggled against him. "You've had your share."

"True, but your brother's accident *and* your dad dying so tragically... Didn't you say you don't see your brother much?"

Her chest tightened. "Yes. Even though he came around to realizing that I wasn't to blame for his accident, we've never been as close as we were before. Even though there's six years between us, he'd always been my protector, looking out for me until the accident."

"And he lost the ability to protect you after that."

"I never thought of it that way." She offered him a smile. "You're good. Maybe you should have been a psychologist."

"I doubt that. It's just common sense, but sometimes it's hard to see reality when you are living through a situation."

"I'll pray about it. Do you get along with your older brother?"

"Yeah."

She scrunched her nose. "Jace, you shook your head 'no' at the same time you said 'yeah.' Maybe it's a hazard that comes from attending law school, but they teach body language there."

Creases formed a *V* between his eyes. "We get along okay."

"Why? What happened?"

His Adam's apple bobbed a few times. "He stole my girl and married her."

15

Jace looked away from Syd's wide-eyed expression and raised his hands, surrender-style. "I'm over it. Really. All is forgiven, and it's finished and done with."

"What happened?"

He didn't tell the sordid story to anyone who might meet his brother and sister-in-law someday. But it was looking more and more unlikely he'd see Syd again, though not by his preference. "I met Molly during college. We were on the school's rodeo team—she was a barrel racer. She'd come home with me a few times on weekends, but Corey was at school in Colorado and they never met. Then, over Easter during our senior year, when I took Molly home for the long weekend, Corey was there.

"A month later, Molly confessed she'd spent time with my brother that weekend when I was off tending to my horse and ranch chores. Over the previous month, they'd emailed and talked on the phone every day. She broke up with me, and right after graduation, she moved to Colorado. A year later, they were married. I'd planned to propose on our graduation day."

The wariness in Syd's eyes changed to compassion. "Isn't there some kind of unwritten code about guys not dating their brother's girlfriends?"

A memory of the hurt and anger he'd felt back then resurfaced. "In a perfect world, I suppose there is. But this world is made up of imperfect human beings."

"Family gatherings must be *awkward*."

"It was especially uncomfortable during their wedding. It's not so bad now, though."

"Do you see each other at rodeos? Is Molly still a barrel racer?"

"After she moved, she competed in a different rodeo circuit. I only ran into her once or twice. She quit when they married. Now she's strictly a full-time mom."

"It sounds like rodeos are like any other subculture. Lawyers get to know other lawyers through conferences and people moving around through the courts. I'm always crossing paths with attorneys I knew in law school."

"True. And within the rodeo culture are different groups—the bull riders who branch out into bull-riding organizations like the PBR, the stock contractors, the bullfighters, the clowns, and the broadcast side."

He stretched out his legs. "All our lives, Corey and I competed against each other in almost everything. In rodeo, I'd get the better scores, but in school, he always got the higher grades and worked at it half as much as me. I thought our competitive days were over when he went to med school and I continued to rodeo and help with the ranch. I never dreamed he'd win over my girl's heart, but he did."

Sydney kept her compassion-filled eyes on him. She looked as if she was about to cry—not a reaction Jace had expected. "Are you sure you don't still care for Molly?" she asked.

"I guess we always have a warm spot for our first love in life, but I'm over it." He felt a smile filling his face as his thoughts changed direction. "They've got two of the cutest kids. It's a blast taking Grayson and Amanda on horseback rides when they're in town." He glanced at Sydney, who had shifted and was staring off at the vending machines. He loved her turned-up nose, her full, pouty lips, and her long lashes. Not to mention the tangle of loose honey-blond curls spilling out of her ponytail. And he loved her tender heart for kids, like what she exhibited with that Down syndrome girl the other night. The loyalty she showed to her mom and to her dad's memory spoke volumes also. He'd have to pray for her to heal the chasm with her brother.

The door to the hall opened, and they both jumped. An older woman carrying a small box of tissues stepped in with a nurse and took a seat on the far side of the room.

"A surgeon will be here after the operation to talk to you, Mrs. Hutchins."

The woman nodded. "Thank you. I'll be fine."

Jace slumped into the cushion. He'd nearly forgotten that this wasn't their private room. Just as well. With company, they wouldn't be tempted to kiss any more or continue baring their souls.

Syd rested her head on his shoulder and he nuzzled his face in her hair, inhaling the fruity scent. Snuggling with her in the middle of the night in a hospital waiting room felt as natural as riding a horse. If only she could be part of his life every day. He kissed the top of her head and whispered, "Sleep well."

"I'm not sleeping. Just enjoying the cuddle." But within a few minutes, her steady breathing told him she'd dropped off. There was no way he could sleep with Clint on the operating table, though. He'd just rest his eyes until Dr. Cassidy came.

"Jace McGowan?"

Who was calling him? He needed to finish his ride.

"Mr. McGowan. The surgery is over." Someone shook his shoulder.

Jace woke up. He wasn't on a bull after all. He rubbed his eyes and refocused. A bald man wearing blue scrubs stood in front of him with a surgical mask hanging loosely around his neck. Jace yawned as Sydney stirred and slipped out of the circle of his arm.

The man stepped back. "You are Mr. McGowan, correct?"

"Yeah. Jace McGowan. Do you have news on Clint?"

"I'm Dr. Everhart." He pulled over a chair and sat. "We managed to repair Clint's wound and inflate the lung. It will be touch-and-go for the next twenty-four hours. We also set his broken leg and have it in a temporary cast. After the swelling goes down, he'll get a permanent cast. He'll need to stay here for five to seven days. I've been told he lives on your ranch. Will you be able to stay in Robinson and get him back home?"

Jace nodded. "I'll do whatever is necessary."

"Good. He'll be in recovery for several hours. No need for you to stick around. Get some sleep and come back later this morning." He handed Jace a card. "Here's a code number to use when you call for an update."

The doctor left and Jace glanced at Syd. She looked adorable as she rubbed sleep from her eyes.

"What time is it?" She pulled a contact case and a small bottle of solution from her purse and began popping the lenses into her eyes.

"I don't remember you taking your contacts out."

"I did it in the ladies' room. You were asleep. What time is it?"

He glanced at the wall clock. "It's ten after four."

She returned the contact case to her purse, then took out a small mirror and peered into it. "I look awful." She wet her pinky finger and ran it across an eyebrow.

Jace laughed. "You look mighty fine to me."

"My mascara is smudged, I ate off all my lipstick, and most of my hair is out of the elastic. You have a weird definition of 'mighty fine.' " She pulled the band from her hair before gathering up her mass of blond waves and corralling her locks into a new ponytail.

Jace stood, took her by the hand, and tugged her to her feet. He slipped his right arm around her waist and gave her a hug. "You know the old saying, 'Beauty is in the eye of the beholder.' And I behold you as looking mighty fine."

A worried look crossed her face, and she glanced at the lady who'd joined them earlier. She too had dozed off. "Jace, I know what you're hoping for," she whispered. "But I can't stay down here any longer, and flattery will get you nowhere."

If she hadn't said that with a smile on her face, he would have been disheartened. "I'm sure your mother would understand if you waited to leave until Monday morning. If you leave early enough, you could be at your mom's for lunch."

"You don't understand." She gathered up her purse and jacket, then handed him her car keys. "Why don't you drop me off at the hotel and drive my car back to the arena? You can pick me up later."

He pocketed the keys. "Good idea. Now tell me what I don't understand."

She faced him with rigid features. "I haven't missed a Labor Day with Mom since Dad died. I go over there for breakfast and we spend the entire day together. To take away even half would hurt her."

Sydney pulled the door open and stepped into the hall. Using the pace she'd used while walking the streets of Chicago, she headed toward the exit.

Jace hurried to catch up. "Why didn't you say that before?"

She continued walking, not saying a word.

They stepped outside and he gripped her elbow, causing her to stop. "What's going on, Syd? What else aren't you telling me?"

She clutched her throat and met his stare with one of her own. "What I'm not telling you needs to remain unsaid. If plans are still in place for the challenge later today, I'm good to go."

"As am I. Let's get you back to the hotel so you can rest."

16

Jace leaned against the Prius's front left fender while waiting in front of the hotel. Sydney emerged through the glass doors, and he smiled at the sight of her in a ball cap, jeans, a T-shirt, and her borrowed boots. She always looked great, but today's look, with her ponytail pulled through the back of the cap, was his favorite. Especially when accompanied by that beautiful smile.

Grateful that the defensive attitude she'd dumped on him when they left the hospital just hours ago appeared to have vanished, he hurried around to the driver's side and opened the door. Instead, she went to the passenger side and flashed him another heart-stopping smile. "You may as well drive since the seat is already adjusted to you." Without waiting for him to come around to do the gentlemanly thing, she opened the door and slid onto the passenger seat.

After they'd traveled in silence through downtown Robinson, he glanced at her briefly as he drove. "Did you get coffee at the hotel? There's the Java Hut up here. We could—"

"I'll take a double-shot vanilla latte."

He burst out laughing. "Well, I guess the lady wants some caffeine."

"Do they serve it intravenously? You do realize that you only dropped me off four hours ago, right?"

He yawned. "Seems like a lifetime. I think I slept so hard in the two or three hours my head was on the pillow that I packed in six."

"You should teach how to do that. You'd make millions, and your money problems would be over."

After he gave their order at the drive-through, he looked over at her. "I stopped by the hospital already. Clint's doing okay. He's groggy but awake. He chewed me out for keeping you in the waiting room with me half the night."

The corners of her mouth lifted. "What a sweet guy. I hope you told him I chose to stay. Does he know you're planning to hang around to drive him home when he's released from the hospital?"

Jace shook his head. "Nah. He was too groggy. If I'd told him, I'd have to repeat it later anyway. We can stop by the hospital after you fail your challenge." He grinned. "Truthfully, I hope you don't fail. I want you to be able to ride again and enjoy it."

"You remember that if I stay on for five minutes, you'll need to renegotiate the contract."

"Yep."

She handed him a ten-dollar bill. "Here come our drinks."

He pushed her hand away. "Let me get this."

"I'm sure your uncle won't mind paying for our morning coffee."

The woman behind the window handed Jace their coffees, and Jace handed her a ten from his wallet before asking for a receipt. They sipped in silence while Jace did a search on his phone for a nearby park. The woman returned to the window and Jace pocketed the change and receipt. Putting the car in gear, he said, "We have a few minutes. Mind if I find a place to pull off and talk?"

"Okay."

He made a left out the Java Hut's driveway and drove a short distance before turning left again. "I think there's a lagoon down this way—and hopefully a place to sit a bit." He spotted the water off to his right and drove up next to it. "Not exactly like the Wabash, but this will do." He shut off the motor and faced her. After the conversation they were about to have, this could be the last time they'd be alone together. It all depended on her response. "I'm confused, Syd."

She turned toward him. A frown marred her face. "Confused?"

"Yeah. While we bared our souls in the waiting room, I got the sense that you were letting down your walls and maybe agreeing to give a relationship with me a chance. That's the only reason I brought up the possibility of your staying longer. One minute you're cuddling with me, and the next you're racing down the hall as though you can't get away fast enough. Then this morning, you're all smiles and friendly. You've got my head spinning faster than a rank bull. Your turn." He took a swig of his double-shot coffee and waited while Syd stared into her latte, which she held with both hands.

He was about to say something when she raised her head and looked at him with watery eyes. "Jace, I don't know what to say except that I'm sorry."

He drained the rest of his coffee and crumpled the paper cup. "Why you run hot and cold on me would be a good start. I sense you're attracted, the same as I am to you, but when your feelings start to deepen, you panic and run. Am I correct?"

"That about sums it up."

"Maybe if I knew why, I'd understand."

Sydney looked at her watch. "It will take more time than we have to explain."

Jace glanced at the dash clock and wished he hadn't agreed to teach the class. He started the motor and put the car in gear. "After the challenge, the floor will be yours."

She offered him a closed-lip smile. "Thanks. I think."

At the arena, Jace parked the Prius next to the rig as his cousin walked up, bringing Charley with her. "There's Lacy with my horse. I need to hightail it over to the arena. You'll be on Shiloh. She's a gentle spirit when she's not running barrels. I need to use Charley for the first part of the clinic; then Lacy's going to ride him while you're on Shiloh."

"I'd love to watch you teach while we wait, if that's okay with you."

He frowned. *There she goes again.* "Why?"

She shrugged. "I've seen your eyes light up whenever you mention the class. I want to see why it brings you so much joy. Working with kids seems the polar opposite to beating a dangerous animal at his game."

He'd never thought of it that way before, and he loved it. "Sure. Why not."

Lacy handed him Charley's reins, and he mounted the horse. "I'll see you gals over there." He trotted him through the open gate and into the arena.

Sydney's gaze followed Jace as he rode his horse at a gallop around the arena. The minutes to be with the man were fast dwindling. Parting would be anything but sweet, but the ache wouldn't be anything close to the pain she went through with Ryan. Best to end things now.

She looked at Lacy. "I need to make a quick call. If you want to head down to the clinic, don't wait for me."

Lacy said she'd wait, and Sydney stepped away, tugging her cell phone from her jeans pocket as she walked. She knew the chances of getting a connection were slim, but she sure could use a quick talk with Erin. She stared at the phone's screen—no connection. Sydney sighed and stuffed the phone back into her pocket.

Lacy stood looking into the arena when Sydney returned. She followed Lacy's gaze to where Jace sat atop Charley at the other end of the dirt. A small group of adults and children had already gathered nearby, while others continued to arrive.

Several cowboys entered the arena from a gate opposite to where she and Lacy stood, each leading a horse toward the clinic area. Feelings Sydney hadn't experienced in years rose to the surface. Trusting herself enough to get on a horse again and ride with the wind in her hair would be wonderful. If she did well, maybe she and Erin could start riding together.

"Looks like the kids and parents are gearing up for the clinic. We'd better walk down there," Lacy said.

Sydney walked beside her. "I'm looking forward to watching how Jace teaches such young children. He said I could observe the class. It won't disturb Jace that we're here, will it?"

"He'll be too focused on what he's doing to even notice."

She and Lacy walked along the edge of the arena until they came to the group in front of the timed-event chute. Jace had dismounted and was explaining how they would first work with horses and then, for the more advanced riders, go into the elementary process of learning to rope using a dummy calf. He asked for kids ages ten through twelve to come forward to ride the horses first, and three boys and a girl ran up to him. Several of the younger children started to fuss to their parents about not being chosen first. In a gentle tone of voice, Jace told the younger children they'd have more time with him after the older kids started working on roping with the other instructors.

After the kids had been helped onto the horses, Jace mounted Charley and started leading them in a circle around the arena.

"We're not leaving, Colton. You've done nothing but talk about this class for days. It'll be fun."

Sydney glanced over at a boy who looked to be around seven and was on the verge of tears. "I can't, Dad. I'm scared."

The dad looked exasperated. "Mrs. Henry said that riding horses would help build your confidence."

Colton crossed his arms and shook his head. His lower lip protruded like a tiny shelf.

Sydney took a step toward the pair and then stopped. What was she doing? Her days of working with such kids had passed with her dad. She had no claim to know how to help the boy.

The boy's face had turned as red as the bandanna he wore, and the dad appeared ready to give in. Jace and his charges were beginning a second circle of the arena—time enough to offer assistance. Even if she helped a teensy bit, she might be able to turn the situation around. Sydney approached the boy and his father. "Excuse me... Maybe I can assist."

The dad relaxed. "I'll take any help I can get. Are you with the rodeo?"

"No. But I know the instructor of the clinic and I've had some experience with children and their fears of riding." She stuck out her hand. "I'm Sydney Knight."

The man shook her hand. "Tom Mulligan." He looked down at his son. "This nice lady is going to help you."

Sydney pulled the soft tone of voice she hadn't used with kids in years out of the mothballs and hunched down, bringing her eyes level with the boy's.

"Colton, isn't it?"

He nodded.

"That's a cool name. I'd be happy to help you get on a horse and ride him. What do you think?"

Colton looked across the arena at Jace and the other kids. "I'm scared. These horses are a lot bigger than the ones at the pony ride."

"They do look big, don't they?"

The dad scowled. "Look, I don't know. Maybe it's better to wait for the instructor. Colton's got an I.E.P. at school and…"

Sydney straightened and stepped away from the boy. As she'd hoped, Mr. Mulligan came with her. "I used to work with a therapeutic horse trainer, and although I'm not certified nor are any of these horses trained, I think some of the techniques used might help your son. A lot of kids with Individual Education Plans come through that program. After he's on the horse, you're welcome to take over and walk alongside him."

The man's eyes widened and he shook his head. "I don't have a clue about horses. I'm fine with you walking with him."

He's really nervous. Probably why Colton is so anxious.

The father gave a nervous laugh. "You may know more than that cowboy out there."

Sydney followed the man's gaze to Jace, who was talking to one of the boys. "He knows his stuff."

A few minutes later, Jace brought the four riders in and the kids dismounted. Jace remained on Charley. Sydney approached him, leading Colton by the hand. She peered up at Jace, careful to hold tightly to the boy's hand while standing so close to the horse. "Jace, this is Colton. He's never ridden before and is a little nervous. Which horse would you suggest he use? I told him I'd walk alongside while he rides. His dad gave permission."

Jace's eyes widened. "Oh. Okay." He dismounted and looked over at the horses. "Hey, Brad, bring your horse over here."

The cowboy led the small quarter horse over. Sydney ignored Jace's stare and rubbed the horse's nose. "What's his name?"

"Max." The cowboy looked at the boy. "You gonna ride him, partner?"

Colton half hid behind Sydney's leg.

Sydney rested a comforting hand on the boy's back. "Yes. He's going to ride, and I'll walk beside him."

Brad looked at Jace with a questioning expression.

"Do as she says." Amusement laced the tone in Jace's voice. He walked over to the boy, bent, and placed his hands on Colton's hips. "Let me help you up into the saddle and get your stirrups adjusted. Then Ms. Knight here will take you around."

The boy appeared to relax at Jace's softened tone and nodded. Jace lifted him into the saddle. Sydney went to the opposite side of the horse and rested a hand on the boy's waist. "You're doing great, Colton. There's nothing to be afraid of."

Jace came around to her side to adjust the other stirrup and whispered in a singsong voice, "I hope you've not been playing me like a fiddle."

"You don't see me sitting on Max, do you?"

"Nope, I sure don't." He went on to check the stirrups of the other children who had already been helped onto their mounts. It looked as if all the other parents were planning to walk beside their children's horses. She hoped none were as nervous as Colton's dad. Jace climbed back on Charley, and at his signal, the children and their horses fell in behind him. Sydney and Colton brought up the rear.

Working to keep her voice even and soft, she gave instructions to Colton on how to hold the reins. They took off at a slow pace, and he handled it well. Halfway around the circle, she let go of the horse's harness. Colton continued to manage the horse with ease while Sydney talked him through the ride. She was amazed at how the phrases the trainer had used came back to her.

After they brought the horses to a halt, Colton said he'd be fine without her, so Sydney joined the other adults as they left the kids and horses to Jace.

Relieved that Lacy didn't pepper her with questions while they watched the rest of the class on riding, Sydney worked to gather strength for what was sure to be a barrage of new questions from Jace. She needed to pray and to talk to Erin. She turned toward the open gate. "Tell Jace I'll meet him by the—"

"No time for me to tell him anything. He's heading this way."

Sydney followed the direction of Lacy's pointing finger.

Jace strode toward them, Charley's lead in one hand and the other fisted. Under the weight of his hard stare, Sydney wanted to disappear.

He stopped and handed Lacy Charley's lead, his eyes never leaving Sydney. "I'm beginning to think that working with Lacy isn't necessary after all."

"Please don't judge until you've heard me out."

"It's a little hard not to judge, Syd. The way you handled Colton and talked him out of his fear... I have questions, so you'd better be thinking of answers. I'll be done here in about forty-five minutes. I'll see you over by the rig." He turned and strode away. Small dusty puffs exploded around his boot heels with every step.

17

The women walked away from the arena in silence, with Charley clip-clopping behind them. Sydney folded her arms against her roiling stomach. She'd expected Jace to be disappointed but not over-the-top honked off. She should have been up front with him. They reached the pens, and Shiloh bobbed her head from where she stood behind the railing. Lacy handed Charley's lead to Sydney and strode to the fence rail. Sydney patted the horse's neck gently.

An ache swelled in Sydney's chest. She'd lost so much she loved just by walking away from the only part of her life that consistently gave her peace. She'd always considered her love of horses a gift from God, but Dad's accident had made her question that assumption. She was one confused and mixed-up girl back then. She might not have Jace at the end of this weekend, but maybe it wasn't too late to bring horses back into her life.

She rubbed Charley's nose absently, then ran her fingers through his soft mane, admiring the good care Jace gave him. The way a man treated his horse said a lot about him. A vision of the hurt she'd seen in Jace's eyes a few minutes ago flashed into her thoughts—hurt she'd put there. So unnecessary, if she'd only told him the whole story from the beginning.

"Since you apparently know your way around horses and handled that little boy with no fear, I'm not sure what we're supposed to do here." The edge to Lacy's voice made the weight of guilt press harder against Sydney's heart.

She looked up. Lacy stood a few feet away, watching and waiting for an answer. Sydney stared at her feet and prayed for the right words. "I stopped riding when my dad died, and I haven't been on a horse since. It's one thing to help a boy through his fear and walk beside a horse, and it's another to sit on one. I've been away from riding for so long, I'm scared to death to get in the saddle again."

Lacy's facial expression softened. "Does Jace know this?"

"Yes. In so many words."

"Then why is he upset?"

"I intentionally left out how experienced I am. If he knew my level of past experience with horses and saw we had that in common, it would be harder to convince him that we can't be together. It seemed the less he knew, the better. It sounds pretty lame, doesn't it?"

Lacy's right brow arched. "Jace said that if you can convince him to renegotiate the contract with Frisky's, Uncle Harry promised you a position on a trial."

Heat rode up Sydney's neck and into her face. "Partially true. I tried to get out of coming down here, and Harry used the temptation of assigning me to a trial as a bargaining chip. I admit that I was enticed, but the real reason I came was my concern for Jace. He needs to renegotiate the contract. Too much is at stake. The ranch, his reputation, his family's welfare... If his attorney won't negotiate a cancellation, I plan to offer to do it pro bono."

Lacy puffed her cheeks and let out the trapped air. "Jace can be a knothead, that's for sure. He doesn't hold his anger for long, though. Hopefully he'll listen when you explain. Meanwhile, let's give it a test before he gets here. I'll saddle up Shiloh for you."

"Thanks, but I'll probably be okay on Charley. We've been getting acquainted." She rubbed the horse's forehead.

Lacy dug into her jeans pocket and held out a fisted hand. "Here's a couple of treats. Give him these, and he's your BFF. But keep them hidden until you're ready to give them, or you'll live to regret it."

They made the covert exchange and Lacy jogged back to Shiloh's pen.

Sydney stroked Charley's forehead, speaking in a soothing tone of voice at the same time. The horse pressed his head into her hand, much like Honey used to do. Tears pricked her eyes as she pulled out the treats. Charley had them gone in a nanosecond.

"Okay, Charley, I'm going to adjust the stirrups so we'll be ready for a ride when Lacy and Shiloh get here."

She was adjusting the second stirrup when Jace ambled up. She tensed and focused on the gate to the arena just over his shoulder. "Is it time already?"

"Yep. Why are you adjusting his stirrups?"

"I told Lacy there was no need for her to switch horses."

His face twisted into a grimace. "I was right. I have been played."

"No, Jace, not played. I really haven't been on a horse since Dad died."

He folded his arms across his chest. "Why don't you fill in the blanks—*if* you can remember them?"

Sydney hated his mocking tone. She glanced toward the pens. Shiloh was saddled, and Lacy sat on the pen's top railing. She was giving them space.

Sydney looked up at Jace's flinty expression. "I was given a pony when I was seven. My dad loved horses and always kept one at a stable outside of town. I took to riding, and within a year, I was ready to move up to a quarter horse. I learned dressage and rode English until high school, when Dad gave me Honey and I switched to Western. I was starting to learn barrel racing the same year Dad died." Her bottom lip trembled, and she bit down on it. "I never rode Honey or any other horse again. Mom kept her until I graduated from high school, but then she sold her." She looked at Jace. His face was blurry. "I still miss her."

"You never rode again?"

"I tried. Even got Honey saddled up ... but I couldn't bring myself to mount her."

Jace handed her a handkerchief, still folded and unused, from his back pocket. "Why didn't you tell me all this before?"

She dabbed beneath her eyes. "I figured the less you knew about my history with horses, the less you'd see us as having anything in common. Today was a game changer, helping Colton and seeing how much I remembered. I need to bring horses back into my life."

"What exactly did you recall that helped that kid?"

"I worked as an assistant to a therapeutic horse trainer during high school and loved it." She looked off into the distance as fresh tears filled her eyes. "I planned to major in child psychology and then make therapeutic horse training my career, but Dad's accident changed all that."

"And now you're going to try riding again." He cocked his head as his lips lifted into a smile. "You sure you remember how?"

Sydney allowed herself a tiny smile. "I didn't forget how to coach Colton, so I don't think I'll have forgotten much."

Jace drew her into a hug. "I'm glad I found this out now. No matter what comes of your life down the road, pray before you give up something you enjoy. It just may be that God wants to use what you love to help others."

At the hopeful tone in his voice, Sydney stepped out of his embrace. "Please don't think this will change our relationship. There are too many obstacles."

"What makes you so sure? Maybe God has other plans." Jace removed his Stetson and scratched his head. "You know, there's a passage where God is talking and says His thoughts aren't our thoughts and, likewise, His ways. What if God means for us to be a couple? Do we want to go against His will?"

The man knew how to knock down every argument. But love meant taking risks that she had no desire to face. "If it *were* His will, wouldn't He have made the way straight by now?"

"It's all about perspective, isn't it? My way looks clear, while yours seems to be riddled with obstacles."

She shrugged. "All the more reason not to force what isn't meant to be." She paused and then said, "One more thing. After I win this challenge, if your lawyer won't help you renegotiate, I'll do it pro bono."

His brows shot up. "Pro bono?"

She stared at the ground and blinked at unbidden tears. "It's the least I can do. I'm really sorry, Jace, for hurting you."

Silence fell between them. Why didn't he say something? Lacy had said he didn't hold his anger long, and he already seemed to have cooled down. *Lord, if he doesn't forgive me, I don't know what I'll do.*

He drew her under the crook of his arm. "I already forgave you minutes ago, but I know you need to hear the words. You are forgiven, Sydney. Now, let's get this over with." He waved Lacy over.

Lacy led Shiloh across the grass and handed the lead to Jace. Her face expressionless, she looked first at Sydney and then at Jace. "I'll be in the trailer taking a nap."

Sydney grabbed Lacy by the arm. "Lacy, I've apologized to Jace and he's forgiven me. I hope you will too."

The barrel racer stared at her boots, then raised her head. "You don't owe me an apology. Far as I can tell, you've been straight with me. But when my kin has been hurt, I hurt, and seeing that Jace has forgiven you, I don't hurt anymore."

Sydney managed a smile. "Thank you, Lacy." She grabbed Charley's reins and raised her left foot to the stirrup. "I may as well get on this boy and prove I can still ride."

Lacy held out her horse's reins. "Take Shiloh. That way Jace can ride with you. You can do this."

Sydney took her foot out of the stirrup and looked at Jace. "I'm game if you are."

"Then let's do it."

A country-western tune filled the air, and Jace winced as he pulled his phone from his shirt pocket. He looked at the screen. "It's the hospital." He swiped his finger over the display. "Jace McGowan. Yes. No. Okay. Yes. Bye." He disconnected and looked from Sydney to Lacy. "Plans have changed. Clint's bleeding somewhere inside, and they need to do emergency surgery to find the source. I have to get over to the hospital ASAP."

18

Sydney pulled up to the hospital's drop-off entrance and Jace pushed open his door. "I'll probably be in the same waiting room from last night." He slammed the door without another word and raced toward the entrance.

Sydney turned into the parking lot and let out a huge sigh. *Nothing like being used.* He'd presumed she'd drive him to the hospital and now, without even thanking her for bringing him, assumed she'd wait with him again while Clint was in surgery. She hated being taken for granted. He could call her when he was ready to leave. Her hotel bed was waiting.

She headed for the exit to the street and braked. *Way to go, Sydney, acting like everything revolves around you. His best friend, who almost died last night, is back in surgery. That's where his mind is now. Grant him some grace.* She'd likely forget her manners, too, if it were Erin in trouble. She drove back into the lot, parked the car, then leaned her forehead on the steering wheel.

"Lord, I don't deserve to have You answer a single one of my prayers, but here I am. I need You. Please forgive my selfish attitude and help me to be an encouragement to Jace. Clint is like family to him, and he's hurting."

She ended her prayer and made a move to collect her purse, but suddenly returned to her prayer position. "God, ever since I helped Colton this morning, I can't get out of my mind the joy I felt while working with him. Do I dare think that someday I can have my dream back?" A vision of working with a special-needs child as she helped a little girl mount a horse and took her through a session emerged in her thoughts. She pressed her palm against her chest in an effort to still her racing heart. God seemed to be saying, "Yes. Pursue your dream. Now is the time."

"But what about my legal work, Lord? I'm almost at the place in the firm when I can finally focus on Dad's legacy." She waited for more words to come or a settling of peace over her.

When nothing happened, she said, "Amen" and grabbed her phone. She had two bars. Enough for a call—maybe.

On the fifth ring, Erin's voice came on. "Hi, this is Erin. I'm probably going crazy with wedding prep or trying out a new recipe so I don't kill my new husband or doing something as mundane as working. Leave a message and I'll get back to you as soon as I can."

Sidney laughed and shook her head. Sometimes she wished she could be as spontaneous as to leave a lighthearted message like that. "Hey, girlfriend, I really, really need to talk to you. I'm going to be in a no-cell-connection zone soon, so please let me know when is a good time to call."

Sydney stepped into the surgical waiting room as Jace tossed a magazine onto an end table. He stood, and their eyes met. "I don't know anything yet. A nurse said she'd notify the surgeon that I'm here. Back to the waiting game. Let's sit over there." He headed toward the couch they'd occupied before.

Sydney dropped beside him. "Sorry I took so long. I stopped to pray."

"I've been praying too. At least they discovered the blood loss before it was too late."

A sinking feeling filled Sydney's stomach. She hadn't prayed for Clint earlier. How selfish was that? "Why don't we pray for Clint right now?"

"Good idea." After taking her hand, Jace bowed his head and his baritone voice filled the room. When he paused after a few minutes of asking for Clint's healing, Sydney spoke her prayers.

After they finished, Jace kept hold of her hand. "I forgot to thank you for driving me over here. To get here otherwise would have meant scrounging around for a car or a truck to borrow or else disconnecting the cab from the trailer."

Feeling duly chastened, Sydney leaned into him. "No worries. Happy to do it."

"Looks like we aren't going to get to do the challenge today. Is tomorrow okay with you?" Jace twisted to look her in the eyes.

"As long as I leave in enough time to be home by early evening."

His forehead creased. "I know how important your Labor Day date with your mom is. We'll make it happen." He let go of her hand and draped his arm across her shoulders. "Tell me about the therapeutic trainer you worked for. What you did with Colton this morning was exceptional. He did great. I loved how his smile never left his face."

Warmth washed over Sydney. "I learned it all by watching my boss. When she saw my interest, she began mentoring me. She told me that my job in assisting her was waiting for me when I was ready to return after my dad's funeral, but I couldn't bring myself to go near a horse and eventually she filled the position. After graduation, I went on to pursue law."

"If you could, would you like to take a stab at becoming a trainer now?"

Had he been hiding in her backseat while she was praying? "I don't know. I've got my law career now. Dad's mission…"

"You said your dad started a legal-assistance group to help addicts. What exactly does it do?"

"Judges are often too quick to imprison drug addicts rather than assigning them a stint in rehab where they can overcome their addiction. Prison only offers more opportunities for drugs, and they can come out as addicted as when they went in. The lawyers who volunteer at the clinic advocate for the addicted so they can get rehab help instead of a prison sentence."

"What led your dad to start the clinic?"

She looked off into the distance to gather her words. "Dad got caught up in the drug scene when he was in college and started dealing to feed his habit. He was arrested his senior year and did a couple of years in prison. He saw with his own eyes what happens once you are inside, and he determined to get out and go to law school to help others like him. It became his passion."

"And he was clean ever since then?"

She nodded. "All that happened before he met my mom. He loved his work. Every time he went to court and managed to sway a judge to send an addict to rehab, he'd come home wearing a huge smile. I'm not sure God allows those who have died to see what their loved ones are doing, but I know if he could see me now, he'd be wearing that same smile."

Silence fell over them a moment and then Jace looked directly at her. "Syd, I don't know anything about lawyering, but I saw that kind of joy on your face when you were working with Colton. I've never seen anything close to that when you talk about your current job—even now. It's fine to not feel the same passion as your dad. Maybe you should rethink things and pray about it. If you don't have the same ambition for law and working with addicts as your dad did, it's okay if…"

"If what?"

He shrugged. "It's none of my business, but it seems to me that you should go after what brings you joy."

The door across the room opened and a man wearing blue scrubs, who looked to be in his midthirties, stepped in. He looked at Jace. "Are you Mr. McGowan?"

Jace straightened. "Yeah, that's me."

The man crossed the room and sat in a nearby chair. "Dr. Springer—the surgeon on duty today. We found the blood vessel that caused Clint's bleed and got it fixed. Your friend is in recovery. You should be able to see him around a half hour, forty-five minutes from now. I'll have a nurse come and get you as soon as he's fully awake."

"Sounds good. Does this affect the prognosis at all?"

The doctor shook his head. "It shouldn't. I read his chart from last night. He ought to be able to travel back to Texas by Thursday or Friday. But each day will tell."

"Thanks. That's good news." Jace stood along with the doctor. "I appreciate all the help Clint's gotten here."

Dr. Springer waved an acknowledgment and reopened the door. "All in a day's work. Happy to do it." The door closed behind him and Jace sat down again.

Sydney stifled a yawn. "Looks like another spell of waiting. Why don't you drive me to the hotel and bring my car back here? I really need a good long nap."

Jace's brows arched. "I can call Lacy and see if she can round up a car."

Sydney waved a dismissive hand. "Not necessary. I don't plan to go anywhere but my bed and then to the laptop. Take the Prius to the arena and pick me up in the morning?"

"You're not interested in attending the rodeo tonight? I'm in the roping event."

She shook her head, thankful that she had a real excuse to miss it this time. "Interested, yes, but I can't with the work waiting for me."

"Okay. Tomorrow morning, we'll go to breakfast and then to cowboy church. After that, the riding challenge."

She quirked her head. "What's 'cowboy church'?"

"Lots of rodeos put on services for the contestants. The one here is held in a small amphitheater in the woods near the campers. It's open to anyone who wants to attend."

Sydney nodded. "Sounds nice. I assume the dress code is jeans and boots?"

He grinned. "Anything goes, but no red high heels."

Sydney gave him a playful punch in the arm. "And what if I decide to wear them?"

He grabbed her fisted hand and opened it before threading their fingers together. "Suit yourself, but you'll be riding the horse barefoot if you do."

"Maybe I should go without the saddle too. Haven't ever ridden bareback."

"It's fun. Once you get back to riding and have your own horse, you'll have to try it."

A sudden vision of riding bareback while galloping through a meadow in the warm summer sun, her hair lifting in the breeze, warmed Sydney.

He squeezed her hand. "What are you smiling about?"

She blinked. "I was imagining what it would be like to ride bareback. It probably won't happen in my lifetime."

He stood and tugged her to a standing position. "Nothing is impossible with God."

They headed for the hospital's main exit. At the door, they met up with a young woman riding in a wheelchair and holding an infant. The nurse pushing the wheelchair halted as a man swung the door open from outside. A grin split his face. "Okay, honey, I've got the infant seat secure in the backseat. We're ready." He looked at his wife, and Sydney could see the love radiating toward her and their baby.

Sydney and Jace waited until the group was through the door to exit. As they walked past, she watched the new dad get the baby situated before he assisted his wife into the backseat next to their new child.

Yearning filled Sydney's heart, and she willed it away. She should get her mind on the work waiting for her back in her room.

Jace dropped Sydney off at the hotel after a quick hug good-bye.

In the hotel room, she decided to soak in the jetted tub one more time before napping. After sliding into the bubbling hot water, she leaned back and let out a sigh. Her thoughts went to the young couple with their new baby. By now they were probably home and getting settled, maybe showing off the baby to their family. A vision of being married to Jace and having a child with him flowed into her mind. She and Ryan had often talked about the family they would raise together and how she could balance her work at the clinic along with motherhood. All of that fizzled the morning of her non-wedding.

If Ryan had been the only man in her life to prefer another woman over her, maybe she wouldn't be so fearful of taking a risk with Jace. But before Ryan, there was Logan. They'd met in the university law library and become study partners. He was nerdy but good-looking, and it wasn't long before they became almost joined at the hip. She'd never expected him to be anything but faithful until the day she received an e-mail from a woman in the law office where he was clerking, saying that Logan was heavily involved with one of the female attorneys there. A married one. Sydney confronted him that evening and he admitted to everything.

Jace had lost his girl to his own brother and yet he seemed willing to take a risk at love again. But then, he took a risk every time he got on a bull.

God might give her a second chance at working with horses and kids, but would He give her a   at love with Jace? Would Jace understand if she told him the complete reason why they couldn't be together? Maybe, maybe not. Either way, she was certain he would try to talk her into taking a risk, and she wasn't sure she was ready to do that. Not even for Jace.

19

Sydney tucked her red heels into her suitcase and giggled at the memory of trying to walk through the grass in them. Jace had been a good sport, when most guys would have probably agreed to negotiate just to get the wacko lawyer out of town. A wave of regret came over her. She shouldn't be giggling when she had no idea how Clint was doing. He seemed okay when they left him yesterday, but conditions like his could reverse quickly.

The room phone rang and she walked to where it sat on the nightstand. It had to be Jace, saying he was waiting downstairs.

Tempted to answer with something other than "Hello," she refrained. *Never assume anything.*

"Hey, Syd. I'm here in the hotel parking lot. Are you ready?"

"Just finished packing. How is Clint doing? Did you call him?"

"He's fine. I stopped to see him before coming over here. He's in ICU, but he's doing okay and is expected to be in a regular room later today. Crisis averted."

"That's a relief. I've been praying for him."

"As have I. Do you need help with your suitcase?"

"I can manage. The elevator makes it easy. I'll check out and meet you in front."

A few minutes later, Sydney wheeled her suitcase through the hotel's main door. Under the overhang, wearing black jeans, polished black boots, and yet another plaid long-sleeved shirt, Jace leaned against the Prius. When he spotted her, he held up her keys and arched his brows in a question.

Loving how, once again, he didn't presume to be the driver, she waved his proffered hand away. "Do you mind driving? I'll be behind the wheel long enough this afternoon."

"No problem." Jace pressed a button on the fob and the hatch opened. He grabbed her suitcase by the handle and slid it into the cargo area, then closed the hatch and opened the passenger door.

Sydney forced a laugh. "You've spoiled me this week. I'm going to miss that." *And I'm going to miss you too, cowboy.*

Sadness filled Jace's eyes. "I'm going to miss spoiling you. Let's say we pretend we're not saying good-bye later and instead enjoy the morning without that negative thought spoiling our day."

A few minutes later, Jace had the car heading east toward the arena. They hadn't spoken since their exchange at the hotel, and she was grateful. Trying to talk around the growing lump in her throat would be difficult. For as much as she'd been saying she needed to leave and dating was out of the question, now that her departure was imminent, she hated it.

Before leaving Robinson, Jace turned north. "There's a little restaurant over in Hutsonville that I've heard serves a decent breakfast. I hope you're hungry. A couple of ropers told me the servings are large and lip-smacking good—and that's a quote from the guys. They're not exactly professional food critics, but they know their way around a plate of food."

Sydney pressed her hand against her stomach. The thought of a large country breakfast did not sit well. About all her knotted stomach could handle was toast and tea. "The best kind of critic."

"True, but—am I detecting that it's not appealing to you?"

So much for trying to mask her true feelings. "I'm a little off today and can't imagine eating a huge meal right now."

Jace slowed the car. "We can go somewhere else. Want me to turn around?"

Her heart warmed at his consideration, but why spoil his morning because of her jittery stomach? "I didn't sleep well. If I can get tea and toast, I'll be okay."

The right corner of his mouth lifted, assuring Sydney that she'd said the right thing.

"Order whatever you want. I didn't sleep well either. Blew the roping last night—broke the barrier."

"I'm sorry, Jace. I didn't even ask how you did in your event. What does that mean, to break the barrier?"

"No need to apologize. Charley started running before the calf did. There's a thin string called the 'barrier' that breaks when that happens. The calf has to start running before the horse. It's the horse's job to catch up to him."

"Don't you get a do-over like the reride in bull riding?"

"Afraid not. My entry fee went down the drain. But I'm still the top-scoring bull ride. If no one beats my score tonight, I'll win first place in the all-around."

"I'm glad to hear that. You need all the winnings you can get."

"Boy, howdy, you got that right."

A short time later, they passed several of Hutsonville's well-kept yards before coming to a dead end at what appeared to be the town's main street. Ahead, the Wabash River flowed as peacefully and as serenely as it had the other day downriver. Jace took a left and drove past a park that ran along the river's shoreline. The road stopped in front of a small bungalow-type house with a red-and-white awning.

"Is this what you're looking for?"

Jace turned the Prius into an empty spot in front of the eatery. "This is it."

The Wabash Coffee House looked no wider than Sydney's living room back home. But as long as they served good coffee and tea, the size didn't matter. "Who knew a town this small would have a coffee house?"

Jace's dimples deepened. "I thought you'd like it. Sure you only want tea?"

"I think I can manage a hot cup of coffee."

Inside, people huddled over platefuls of bacon and eggs, filling up every mismatched table and chair in the small room. A young man called out from behind a counter, "There's more seating in the back. Go find a table, and someone will be with you soon."

Jace pressed his hand to the small of Sydney's back and called out, "Thanks," as he guided her past shelves of antique bowls, kitchen tools, and old pictures and into another crowded dining room. They sat at one of the two empty tables remaining.

Sydney surveyed the room. Men in bib overalls with John Deere caps on their heads and women in jean shorts or capris and T-shirts jabbered away as they ate. It appeared the entire town had decided to have breakfast out that morning. "I feel like we are in the middle of a dozen different family meals going on in the same large kitchen."

"Good analogy. If the crowd is any indication of the quality of the food, my buddies were right." Jace took two menus from a clip in the center of the table and handed one to her. "Here you go—in case you decide to get something with your toast."

Sydney scanned the room. "This reminds me of the house I grew up in."

"I wondered why you were smiling. How so?"

"My parents collected antiques they found at secondhand stores." Sydney set down the menu and stood. "I want to check out something." She wandered over to a large chest, the only piece of furniture in the room, and ran her hand over its top.

"Nice dresser." Jace came up and tugged open a drawer. He ran his fingers along the sides of it. "Dovetailed. That, I like." He checked the price tag and disappointment clouded his face. "Three-fifty. Can't do it."

Sydney stared at him. He liked antiques. What other boxes under likes and dislikes would he tick off? When she'd made up that list back in college, she'd never dreamed that a cowboy from Texas would have such varied interests.

An older man with thinning gray hair stood up from one of the tables and approached them with a lopsided gait. "The price is a bargain, ya know. The piece came from a wealthy family over in Indy. Worth at least five."

Jace pursed his lips. "Are you the dealer?"

"Owner. It's here on consignment."

"Too much for me right now. I'll have to take a pass."

The man scowled. "Well, I could go three. But no more."

Jace shook his head. "Sorry, but not this time. Thanks."

They returned to their table, and Sydney spread her napkin on her lap. "At first I thought he meant three dollars and then realized he meant three hundred."

"I wish it was three bucks. It's just the thing I've been looking for. But until those taxes are paid and I can get my house construction going again, I can't even buy a stick to furnish it."

Sydney glanced at the choices on the menu, grateful her appetite had returned. She looked up at Jace. "What will your house look like when it's finished? Is it a two-story?"

The lines around his eyes creased as he smiled. "It's one-story, rustic, but with modern touches. Three bedrooms, or four if you count the bonus room over the garage."

The same ache she'd experienced when seeing the new family resurfaced and wrapped around Sydney's heart. Someday Jace would finish his house and fill it with a wife and kids. She never should have asked.

He picked up his menu and studied it. "I have a taste for French toast and a double order of bacon. The one with cinnamon and raisin bread sounds great. Are you going to take a risk and order something other than that spartan breakfast you mentioned?"

His choice of words hadn't gone unnoticed. *If only taking a risk on love were as easy as deciding what to eat.* "I've already decided on scrambled eggs and whole-grain toast."

They gave their orders to the waitress when she came, and Sydney pulled out her phone, grateful to see they'd escaped the cell-phone blackout and she had a connection. She clicked on the weather app to check the report for Chicago. Clear with pleasant temperatures promised a nice ride home. Rain would have better matched her growing mood.

Jace stood and strode into the front room to see if they had a Sunday paper, and Sydney began downloading her e-mail. There were several from Harry ... and one from Erin, saying she'd tried to call her back but the call wouldn't go through. And one from Mom? Sydney frowned. Her mother wasn't a big computer user, and getting e-mail from her usually meant it was urgent. She clicked on the message.

HAVE NEWS TO SHARE. I'VE BEEN TRYING TO REACH YOU BY PHONE

BUT CAN'T GET THROUGH. PLEASE CALL ME BEFORE YOU COME OVER TOMORROW, BUT NOT UNTIL LATER THIS AFTERNOON. MOM

"Not exactly the San Antonio Sunday paper, but then, we're not in Kansas anymore, are we?"

Sydney looked up at Jace as he set a thin tabloid-style newspaper on the table. "Kansas?"

"You know, the line from *The Wizard of Oz.*"

"Oh. Sorry. I was distracted by an e-mail from my mom. She says to call her before coming over tomorrow but not until later today. I wonder why."

"Maybe she's in church this morning."

"Possibly, but the message doesn't sound like her." She dropped the phone into her purse. "Whatever it is, I can't know about it until later. So what's in the news? I'm guessing a lot of agricultural reports."

He glanced at the paper. "There's that, but more. This is a weekly that came out last Thursday. Did you know the big rodeo is in town this weekend?" He grinned, picked up the paper, and turned the page. "They even have a picture of a strange-looking cowboy inside."

Sydney leaned over the table as he held up the paper. A large photo of a cowboy on a bull's back, his face turned away from the camera and his left arm raised, filled the top half of the page. The shirt and chaps looked familiar. "Would the strange-looking cowboy happen to be you?"

He snickered. "Most people wouldn't know if the caption didn't say so. The article mentions the rodeo class for kids I taught yesterday, which I guess is why they used this shot."

She laughed. "I had no idea I was hanging around with a celebrity."

"Only to a very small circle of fans. Anyway, here comes our food."

After Jace said a blessing, silence fell between them while they ate. As Sydney finished her last forkful of eggs, the waitress came up with a pot of coffee. "Refills?"

They both pushed their empty mugs toward her and said yes in unison.

After the server left, Jace took a swig of the steaming brew. "I really need this. I thought I'd sleep like a rock. It surprised me that I didn't."

"I'm not surprised. With Clint's accident, our waiting room all-nighter, and your event last night, I'm sure you were running on adrenaline."

"Maybe, but I think the main problem was you." He stretched his arm across the table and laid his hand over hers, giving it a squeeze.

Her pulse quickened as an electric-like shiver traveled up her arm. She knew she should pull her hand away but couldn't bring herself to do so.

"I'm crazy about you, Syd. Half the night, I couldn't stop thinking about having to say good-bye and possibly never seeing you again."

She opened her mouth but closed it when he made a motion with his free hand to stop her. "Don't, until I finish."

She stared at her lap. She wanted to tell him she was crazy about him too, but the last two times she'd laid out her heart that way, it was squashed like a bug and kicked to the curb like yesterday's garbage.

"Remember what I talked about yesterday?" Jace asked. "Chasing your dream and doing what God called you to do, not what He called your dad to do? Please pray about that. Promise me? I'd like to help—"

Pain filled her throat and she tried to swallow. She couldn't hear any more. She scraped her chair back and jumped to her feet. "Not now, Jace. I need air."

"Syd, wait."

She scurried past the crowded tables in the front dining room and pushed open the door to the outside. Where could she go? She couldn't get in the car. Jace had her keys, and the doors were locked. Ahead, the small park next to the river beckoned like an oasis. She darted across the road and into the park. Inside a picnic shelter, she plopped onto a bench connected to a long table. A couple of moments later, a door slam sounded. She turned and glanced over her shoulder as Jace bolted across the restaurant parking lot. Their gazes locked, and she turned away. He should have understood that she needed to be alone. Just as she was wondering whether she should move farther away to one of those benches facing the water, a hand gripped her shoulder. She twisted around. Worry emanated from Jace's eyes as he studied her face.

Warmth suddenly washed over her. He really cared for her. Maybe it was time to let down her guard. But Logan had made her feel the same way and so had Ryan, right up to their wedding day. Look what had happened with them, and she'd known both a whole lot longer than Jace. She turned away. "Can I have some time?"

"If we're going to make it to church—"

Sydney shrugged his hand off her shoulder. "Just a few minutes." She slid from the table and scurried a short distance away to a park bench that faced the river. After taking a seat, she stared at the water. He'd told her he was falling for her. He wasn't Ryan. She wanted to believe that this time would be different, but every man in her life—Dad, Logan, Ryan, even Nate, in a way—had left her. Why would Jace be different?

"You left your purse."

She looked up.

Jace held out her handbag. Sydney took it and sat it next to her on the bench. "Thank you. I meant to pay the bill."

"All done. Uncle Harry's paid for enough this weekend. My treat. Mind if I sit?"

She slid over and he settled beside her.

"It's time, Syd."

"Time for what?"

"You got a pass yesterday, but no more interruptions. It's time for you to tell me why even if you get over the horse thing and perhaps decide to chase your dream, we still can't see each other again. Let me guess. Uncle Harry will have my hide if I steal you away from him."

"I doubt it. I have a hunch he had ulterior motives in sending me down here."

"Like what?"

"For us to get together, probably. I've been remembering all the times he's mentioned you during the past two years."

"And here I thought he was concerned for my financial future."

"He *is* concerned about the contract, but why would he insist I work with you and come down here? He hinted at knowing that we were drawn to each other. I don't know how he knew. I sure didn't tell him."

"I suspected he wasn't all business." He took both her hands in his, setting off a zillion butterflies in her stomach. "We've got a little wiggle room before the church service. As I said yesterday, the floor is yours."

Sydney closed her eyes and prayed God would tell her what to do. Maybe it was better to tell Jace. Of course, he'd insist he wasn't like the others and would be faithful. But that didn't mean she could trust him. If there was even an ounce of truth in those rumors about him being a player...

She opened her eyes and faced him. "Every man—"A lively jazz tune sounded from Sydney's purse. "That's my mother." She fished her iPhone from her purse and answered. "Hi, Mom. I was going to call later like you'd asked."

"I couldn't wait any longer to tell you my wonderful news."

"What's so great that it couldn't wait? We're going to be together tomorrow."

"That's why it can't wait, honey. I won't be home."

Sydney's chest tightened as silence filled the connection. She checked the screen. They were still connected. "Mom, are you there?"

"Yes. I'm just trying to say this right."

"Do you want to meet elsewhere tomorrow? Where will you be?"

"On my honeymoon. I got married yesterday."

20

A heavy coldness wrapped around Sydney. She held her phone between her chin and her shoulder and hugged herself, but the chill remained. "Married? To who? Is this some kind of a joke?"

"I wouldn't joke about this. I know it's a shock and you've only met Russ once. But he's eager to get to know you."

A tremble began somewhere deep inside Sydney's gut and worked its way up to her lips. "You've only known him a month." Her voice sounded unnatural, strained.

"Have you forgotten that we were high school sweethearts? We've been dating for six weeks now—long enough to know that we love each other. It's different when you're older."

"What about Dad?"

"Your father has been gone a long time. I need to move on with my life. He would want me to. And he'd want the same for you too, Sydney."

"But you did this on the anniversary of his death."

"Not the actual date, which isn't until Wednesday. This was the only time Russ could get away from the office. We took advantage of the long weekend."

"Where are you calling from?"

"I'm in Vegas. We're going on to—"

"Vegas? You? Vegas?"

"There's more to this town than gambling and showgirls. We got married in a small church we found—just the preacher and his wife as a witness. No one else. We'll have a church ceremony and reception later."

Sydney looked toward the river as Jace picked up a stone and skipped it over the water. When had he left the bench? She yearned for him to return. "You may have known Russ in high school, but people change, Mom. He's not the same kid you dated."

"Of course he's changed, and so have I. Both for the better. The best thing is, he's a Christian. Has been for twenty years."

"That's nice." She hated how cold her voice sounded.

"Is that all you can say?"

"I'm just ... trying to take it all in. Isn't Russ from Milwaukee? Will you be moving there?"

Mom cleared her throat. "Actually, Waukesha. A little west of Milwaukee. Russ has his work there. But it's only a short drive up the interstate. We can see each other as often as we do now. You're going to love him. His daughter and her family live an hour north of Milwaukee too. You're gaining a sister. You'll love Julie."

Just one big love fest. An ache filled Syd's chest. She didn't want a sister. She wanted her mother.

"We didn't decide to elope until Tuesday evening and made the arrangements by phone the next morning. I tried to call you on Thursday night and several times on Friday, but I couldn't get through. A couple of times I left a voice mail. Didn't you get it? I did get a hold of Nate and told him. He was surprised too, but—"

"All I've had from you is the e-mail this morning telling me to not call back until this afternoon. I'm on a business trip downstate, and the service here isn't good."

"When I couldn't reach you, I called Harry. He said you were helping him with some legal work involving his nephew, but he didn't say where."

"I'm in a small town for a rodeo his nephew is competing in this weekend. I was planning to return to Chicago later today for our time together tomorrow."

"I'm glad I called now, then. No need to hurry back if you don't have to. Is the nephew nice?"

"Yes. I need to go, Mom. I'll talk to you when you get home."

Sydney disconnected and stuffed the phone into her jeans pocket. She stood and walked to the river's edge a distance down from Jace. She wanted to hate Russ ... what was his last name again? Mom had said it when they were introduced. Michaels? Carmichael? That was it. Carmichael. *Thanks a lot, Russ Carmichael.*

And now another person in her life was moving on. Mom talked as if they'd see each other all the time. Sydney knew what would inevitably happen. It was never intentional, but over time, newlyweds went their own way with their spouses, and soon they were no longer a part of the old inner circle. It wouldn't be long before Erin would be out of Sydney's life too, except for maybe an occasional lunch date.

She squeezed her eyelids shut and willed the pressure at the back of her eyes to lessen. The last thing she wanted to do was cry.

"Want to talk about it?"

She stepped into Jace's outstretched arms. "Mom eloped with her high school sweetheart—whom she's only recently began seeing. She wanted me to know she's on her honeymoon in Vegas and won't be home tomorrow."

He eased away from her gently until their gazes met. "I'm glad I was here. You don't deserve to be hit with news like that alone."

She let her eyes search his face. "Am I selfish for being angry? Maybe *angry* isn't the right word. *Upset* is better." She pressed her face against his chest.

"Maybe *abandoned*?"

"Are you a mind reader?"

"No, but I know how I'd feel if my mom did something like that. Why didn't she call you?"

"She did, on Thursday. And with the less-than-perfect phone service around here, the calls and voice mails didn't go through. She finally called Harry to see if he knew where I was. And she wanted to know if you were nice."

He pressed a kiss to her forehead. "I hope you said I was the nicest guy you've ever met."

She couldn't help but giggle. "I didn't go that far, but I said yes, you are nice."

"Have you met her new husband?"

"Once. He seems okay. He owns a small manufacturing company near Milwaukee. That's about all I know."

"Sounds like she's not only married but also moving to Wisconsin."

"Yes. About an hour or so away, that's all." She looked up at Jace. "How can they think they're in love so fast?"

"Syd, how did we feel after one date?"

"It's not the same."

"Why not?"

"What we felt was only infatuation."

"Infatuation doesn't last two years."

He had a good point. But if she wasn't infatuated with Jace, that only left one possibility to describe what she was feeling. She'd stick with infatuation.

"Don't you agree, Counselor?"

She leaned back and looked into his eyes. "I—

Her phone chimed and she turned away to pull the device from her pocket. "I'd better see what the text message is."

"Can't it wait?"

"What if it's—"

His lips covered hers in a soft, feathery kiss she didn't want to end.

The phone chimed again.

Jace broke the kiss. "Persistent phone you've got there."

Sydney stepped out of his embrace and pressed the text message notification. An image of Mom and Russ—cheek to cheek and holding up their left hands to display their rings—filled the small screen. She handed the phone to Jace. "Now she's sending me pictures."

"They both look like they're crazy in love. Where did they meet up again?"

"At their fortieth high school reunion."

"I hear that happens a lot. And many of the marriages work out." He gave her back the phone.

"I know I should be happy for her, but I feel as if I'm betraying Dad if I share in her excitement."

Jace took her hand, and she let him lead her to the car. As they approached the vehicle, he insisted on driving, and she gladly agreed. In her state of mind, she'd be a danger on the road. After they'd buckled in, Jace faced her. "How many years has it been since your dad's accident?"

"Almost fourteen."

"How do you think he would feel about your mom remarrying?"

A memory of Sydney's grandmother's second marriage popped into her thoughts. Grandpa Knight had died six months earlier, and the family was shocked when Gram announced one day that she was marrying Grandpa's cousin. Sydney had been ten at the time and couldn't understand how Gram could marry a relative. Then Mom had explained he wasn't Gram's blood relative, only a cousin by marriage. Dad had kept a cool head about it and said that if Paul made Gram happy, it was all good. Gram and Paul were married for twelve years until he died from a heart attack. She passed two years later from a broken heart.

"Syd?"

"I think Dad would be okay."

"Then why can't you be too?"

She shrugged. "I don't know. My mom deserves to be happy, even if it means getting married again."

Grateful for the silence that fell between them as Jace drove past the same corn and soybean fields from earlier, Sydney prayed for the right attitude about her mom. There wasn't anything to be done to change the situation, and to make a scene would only cause tension. This was her issue, and she had to deal with it. But did she really want to go back to Chicago this afternoon and sit in her apartment all day tomorrow, brooding?

"No need to go home today, right? Maybe your room at the hotel is still available."

She looked over at Jace. "There you go again."

He gave her a quick glance. "What did I do?"

"You read my mind."

"You know the old saying. 'Great minds think alike.' "

Sydney pulled out her phone, found the hotel number, and tapped the screen. Her room was no longer available, but they could put her in a regular room. No suite. She took it and hung up.

"Lost the suite, but they had an opening in another room."

"So I gathered. I don't think we can make church now, so what do you say we stop at the hospital and see Clint?"

21

It didn't take Jace more than ten minutes to get to the hospital. He glanced around the nearly empty parking lot. "Looks like most people around here spend Sunday morning in worship services. Did you see the full parking lot next to the church back there?"

"I did. I'm sorry I made us miss cowboy church."

How could she be concerned about that, with all she'd just experienced with her mom? He reached over and took her hand. "No worries. It wasn't your fault. Let's see how Clint is doing."

At the main desk, Jace was elated to hear Clint was out of ICU and in a regular bed. After getting directions, they found his room, knocked, and stepped in.

"Hey. I thought you'd be at the service." Clint pressed a button on the remote-like device attached to his bed, and the mattress raised his head a bit higher.

Jace pulled over a chair from the other side of the room, indicated for Sydney to sit, then sat in a second chair. "The schedule changed. And am I glad to see you in a regular room. You had me worried."

Clint shifted positions and winced. "A regular room, but not without the pain of broken bones yet." His gaze went to Sydney. "I thought you were heading north today."

She offered a closed-lip smile. "My plans for tomorrow were canceled, so I decided to stay an extra day."

Clint looked from Sydney to Jace. "What happened with the challenge? What gives?"

"It was interrupted yesterday by my traveling partner having to go into surgery for a second time. We're headed over to the arena after this to watch Sydney attempt to ride Shiloh." He winked at Sydney.

She rolled her eyes. "You don't think I'm going to ride? There is some good in my mom calling off our plans for tomorrow. I can't wait to prove you wrong."

"I hate it when someone cancels with short notice," Clint said.

Sydney grimaced. "She tried to reach me earlier, but the cell service around here wasn't helpful. I'm glad she got through this morning because she eloped to Vegas. I'm not yet over the shock." She stopped talking. It wasn't like her to speak of her personal life with someone she hardly knew, even if he was Jace's best friend. "Sorry ... that's probably TMI."

Clint held up his hand. "Hey, never too much info when you need to talk about something. My mom's been married twice so far and is working on number three. I get it. I think."

Color drained from Sydney's face. "I'm so sorry. I had no idea."

Clint raised his gaze to the ceiling, then brought it back to Sydney. "I'm used to the revolving door by now. There are plenty more who never bothered to get a marriage license at all. But divorce is tough on the kids no matter how old they are."

"My dad died fourteen years ago. Long enough that we should both move on." She looked at Jace and offered him a weak smile.

Jace looked at Clint. "Any word on when they'll let you endure my company for eight hundred miles?"

"The doc is hoping for Wednesday. They need to make sure my breathing is working." He picked up a plastic device from the side table. "When I can blow in this thing and make the ball reach to the top, I'm good to go. I got it halfway a little bit ago. I'll try again this afternoon." He yawned. "Sorry, I don't mean to be rude, but I'm exhausted and you two have a date with a horse."

Jace stood, and Sydney did the same. He rearranged the chairs, then rested a hand on Clint's shoulder. "Take care, dude."

"Thanks. Let me know who wins."

To Sydney's disappointment, Lacy wasn't around when they arrived at the arena. Although Lacy hadn't seemed upset with Sydney yesterday, she still felt the need to reconnect to assure herself that all was okay between them. Lacy's note to Jace said that she and her girlfriend had decided to drive over to Terre Haute to a Western store.

A few minutes later, Jace came out of the trailer carrying a saddle. "I'll take this over by Charley and then come back for Shiloh's."

"I can carry Shiloh's saddle. Show me where it is."

He cocked his head, his eyes twinkling. "Okay."

A few minutes later, walking side by side, each carrying a saddle, Jace cast her a sideways glance. He didn't need to say a word. She saw the pride and hope in his eyes, and she couldn't blame him. But they were running out of time. If only they had more than a long weekend together.

Sydney approached Shiloh, greeting her in a soft tone of voice. The horse bobbed her head. Pleased, Sydney set the saddle on the ground, then gave the animal one of the treats Jace had given her during their walk to the pen. She removed the saddle pad she'd carried over her shoulder and laid it on Shiloh's back before lifting the saddle and placing it on top of the pad. It felt good doing something familiar, something she'd never tired of doing.

She was tightening the cinch when Jace walked over. "You did that as if you'd been doing it all your life."

"It *was* my life until Dad's accident. Are you ready?"

"Let's leave Shiloh in the pen for a while and just take Charley."

She cast him a questioning look. "What am I going to do? Ride Charley while you watch?"

"Kind of." He grabbed Charley's lead, and they walked over to the meadow. Several cowboys were exercising horses. *Great. So much for privacy.*

Jace surprised her by getting on Charley first, then slipping over the back of the saddle and sitting the pad. He held out his hand. "Come on. Get up here with me."

Sydney gaped at him. "No. That's not fair to Charley."

"He's used to me riding double whenever family visits the ranch. We'll only go around the pasture once and not very fast. Let's see if this helps."

Sydney gripped his hand and placed her boot in the stirrup. She pushed off with her other leg and slid easily into the saddle. Jace's arms came around her. "That feel okay to you?"

Who was he kidding? "Which? Your arms around me, or sitting in the saddle?"

He chuckled and held her against him. "Both," he whispered into her ear, sending a shiver down her neck.

"Both feel fine."

"Good to hear."

If they didn't start moving soon, she was going to melt right into the saddle. Was this where the cowboy and his girl rode off into the sunset? "Who's going to hold the reins?"

"You. I'm just the passenger."

And what a passenger you are. She gave Charley a nudge with her heels and made a clicking sound. He started walking in an easy lope.

"You're doing great, Syd."

Of course she was. With him snuggled up to her back, his arms around her, she'd hardly noticed they were on a horse.

After a short distance, Jace let his arms fall away. "Warn me if you're going to speed him up."

"I won't go any faster. Your weight on his withers must be terribly uncomfortable. I don't want to make it worse."

"He's okay, but thanks for thinking of him."

Without the distraction of his arms, Sydney paid more attention to the ride, thrilled at how at home she felt in the saddle. They reached the lap's halfway point and Jace rested his chin on her shoulder. "How are you feeling now?"

"Good, so far, but what am I going to do when you're not behind me?"

"Good question. Let's find out. Charley, whoa."

The horse halted and Jace slid off. He gave the horse a light swat on his hindquarters. "Go easy, boy." The horse started walking.

I'm riding again. What was I afraid of? She nudged her heels against Charley, and he sped up to a trot without any bouncing in the saddle from her—a sure sign of a newbie. It *was* like riding a bicycle. "Welcome home, Sydney Knight. Welcome home." She gave the horse a stronger nudge than before, and he sped up. "Let's show Jace what we can do."

She galloped the horse up to Jace and halted the animal. "Charley's a great horse, but I'd love to have you ride next to me."

His eyes twinkled. "I'm one step ahead of you. I saw Lacy and her friend pull in and called her. She's bringing Shiloh over."

Sydney dismounted, and Jace pulled her into his arms and spun her around, lifting her feet off the ground. "You did it. I'm so proud of you."

Her feet hit the ground, and they remained in each other's arms. "I couldn't have done it without you. But I'm not ready to celebrate just yet. Not until I ride more than once around the meadow." Sydney leaned back and looked up at him as his gaze fell to her mouth. She rose on her tiptoes and brushed his lips with hers. "I'm not sure I went five minutes."

"It was long enough to suit me." He glanced past her shoulder. "Here's Lacy now."

She stepped out of his embrace.

"Hey, I don't mind a little PDA. It's better than arguing." Lacy trotted up on Shiloh and jumped to the ground.

The barrel racer's grin was all Sydney needed to show her that Lacy was no longer annoyed with her. "Thanks for letting me use your horse once more. We're going to go for a short ride, and then you can have her back for good."

"I'm glad you got the monkey off your back. Take your time." She glanced at Jace. "By the look on my cousin's face, a longer ride than you think is in your future."

22

Sydney stepped from the shower and dried off. Coming back to the hotel after they had taken a trail to the river, she'd spent some time alone in prayer, and a new perspective had emerged. God had shown her grace, and she owed Mom the same. She still didn't like the idea of her marrying someone she'd only gotten reacquainted with a few weeks ago, but who was Sydney to criticize when she herself had fallen hard for Jace after such a short time? Mom was widowed young and had been Nate's main caregiver for years before he was able to be on his own. She shouldn't have to be alone for the rest of her life, married only to her memories. Dad would have wanted her to find love again, and Sydney needed to honor that.

A nagging thought still taunted her. Dad was always about taking risks, and if he'd known how fearful she was of the biggest risk she'd ever faced, he'd have told her what he often said: "In the end, we only regret the chances we didn't take."

Maybe in time she could take Dad's advice, but not today. Tonight they'd attend the rodeo to see if Jace won the all-around and say their good-byes, and then she'd leave for home early tomorrow. Back to the law and working toward carrying on Dad's legacy. She waited for the adrenaline rush that usually accompanied looking forward to the day she'd finally be in court, defending someone who desperately needed rehabilitation. None came. Not even an accelerated heartbeat like yesterday during her prayer about chasing her dream.

Sydney got dressed and put her makeup on and still had time to spare before she had to leave for the arena. She sank onto the bed and reached for the television remote to channel surf when the hotel phone rang.

She answered.

"Sydney, I'm glad I caught you."

"Hi, Jace. Are you ready for some good carnival food?"

"My mom just called. My brother, Cole, is in a heap of trouble. I need to fly home ASAP. I just booked a flight out of O'Hare at six fifteen tomorrow morning." He paused. "I hate to ask, but do you mind driving me up there tonight? If it's too much trouble, I'll get a rental car."

Sydney's thoughts whirled in multiple directions. "Of course I don't mind.

Do we leave now or after the rodeo?"

"Now is fine. Probably better."

"Don't you need to stay in case you won the all-around?"

"Lacy can get my check. Or I can pick it up when I fly back later to bring Clint home."

"Okay. It'll only take me a moment to gather my things and check out."

"You sure you don't mind?"

"This must be why I was meant to stay for another day."

When Sydney arrived at the arena, Jace was waiting outside his trailer. He loaded a backpack and brown duffel into the hatch, then slid onto the passenger seat and tossed his hat in the back.

Worry lines, like the ones Sydney saw on his face the night Clint got hurt, splayed out from his eyes and around his mouth.

As they drove down the lane toward the road, Sydney glanced over at the arena once so foreign to her and now so familiar. She mentally said good-bye to the chutes, the stands, and the animals, surprised at how hard it was to leave. But not near as hard as it would be to say good-bye to the cowboy.

They drove through Robinson and into the countryside toward Effingham, where they'd meet up with I-57. Sydney glanced at Jace. He stared out his window with his jaw throbbing. She shifted her attention back to the road. "So what did your brother do that is causing you to leave so fast?"

"He got into trouble last week for a letting air out of school bus tires. He and his buddies were suspended for three days and got a warning from the cops. It seemed to be over, but then yesterday the police showed up at the house. Someone got into the school's computer system and changed some grades. The cops were able to trace the hack job back to Cole's computer."

She looked over at him. "Yikes. No wonder you need to go home."

He fisted his right hand and punched it into his left palm. "He's the one who never got into trouble. Why now?"

She focused again on the road. "Is he going to be charged, or is it still under investigation?"

"Dunno. Mom's got an attorney on the case. She's about to have a nervous breakdown. He's still a minor. Depending on whether the authorities decide to charge him as a minor or as an adult, he may have to go to an alternative high school. The one near us has a bad rep. If he's charged as an adult, he could do time in prison. That makes the alternative school sound like a country club."

"That's a lot to fall on you."

"Yeah. I keep praying I make the right decisions."

"It's probably because of your dad."

"What would he have to do with anything?"

She winced at his sharp tone and made sure to soften her voice. "I didn't mean anything your dad did. Losing a father is especially hard for a teenage boy. I've seen several guys come through the court system in that situation. After their dads died, they did a one-eighty and started getting into trouble. At least your brothers aren't into drugs."

"So far." He let out a long sigh.

After miles of silence, a road sign indicated that Effingham was coming up. Sydney cast Jace a sideways glance. "Shall we look for a place to eat before we get on the interstate? I doubt you've eaten, and you need sustenance."

At his acceptance, they found a family restaurant near the highway and went inside to sit at a booth. Sydney glanced at a clock on the wall. They were about four hours from O'Hare. She'd probably be dropping Jace off around two a.m. He'd have a long wait to board the plane.

"I know what I want." Jace tossed the menu onto the table.

Sydney looked up. "What's that?"

"Cheeseburger, fries, and a Dr Pepper."

"I'm surprised you can eat so much with all that's going on."

"I always eat when I'm stirred up. Calms my nerves."

She closed her menu. "Tomato soup and a grilled cheese is as close as I usually get to comfort food, unless it's chocolate." That got a small smile out of Jace.

Their food came quickly, and between bites, they reviewed the past several days—the afternoon at the state park in Indiana, Jace's big ride on Friday night, Clint's accident and their all-nighter at the hospital—ending with her victory ride earlier. So many good memories, and now it was ending on a couple of huge downers.

Sydney checked her watch. "It's almost ten. We should hit the road. I'll pay for this." She reached for the check that had sat untouched for the last ten minutes.

Jace's hand smothered hers. "There's one subject we haven't discussed yet. It's true confessions time. Me first."

A sinking feeling came over Sydney. In a split second, about a dozen scenarios ran through her mind, and none were good. It sounded like he still expected her to disclose the real reason for not wanting to date him. She knew she needed to but wanted to wait until she was almost ready to drop him off at the airport. "Okay."

"That sounded like a weak agreement, Counselor."

"It's a little hard to agree to stipulations when I'm not sure what I'm agreeing to."

A corner of his mouth lifted into a wry smile. "Bear with me, okay?"

"I'm all ears."

He swallowed hard and took a sip of his drink before setting it on the table. "I led you on by refusing to renegotiate with Frisky's because I wanted to spend more time with you, and the only way to stop you from heading home was to delay agreeing to renegotiate and suggest the challenge. Last Tuesday, I called my attorney in Texas and asked him to start negotiations with Frisky's. I may have to do some behind-the-scenes stuff, but the prospects are looking good for a favorable settlement. The best outcome so far is that I don't have to pose with scantily clad ladies any longer."

Sydney's face heated as she wrapped her hand around her half-full coffee cup. She couldn't believe what she was hearing. He'd messed with her just like the rest of them and was no better than any of the other men in her life. She lifted the cup in her hand. If she followed through, though, she'd be the one looking like a fool. Not a mature response. She set it down again. "You're lucky we're in a public place. I wanted to toss my coffee in your face."

He frowned. "And I would have deserved it. What stopped you?"

"The thought that if I did it, I'd be the one looking like the fool." Her shoulders sagged. "To be honest, I'm relieved you weren't being stupid, like it appeared. I couldn't imagine why you would be so lame as to not renegotiate when you have the tax issue."

"I kept waiting for you to catch on, but you didn't. One more thing. I'm not sure you need to know this, but I'm going to admit to something else. The person who had reservations for the Jacuzzi suite was me. There weren't any openings at either hotel in Robinson."

Sydney reached over and took his hand. "You gave up the suite for a hard old bed in the rig? I didn't deserve that. Not after the way I was with you at lunch that day."

He squeezed her hand. "It was either that or booking you a hotel over in Indiana, and you saw how far the nearest bridges are from Palestine. The bed in the truck cab isn't as bad as you might think. But I did miss that jetted tub after my ride." He punctuated the statement with a wink. "By the way, I never told Harry I did that. Okay. Your turn."

Would he ever stop? Now he was checking boxes she'd never thought of. He was leaving no rock unturned and expected her to do the same, but could she? She stacked their dirty dishes and laid the utensils across the top plate, one beside the other, then lined up the plates at the edge of the table. "You already know about my love of horses, my dream to be a therapeutic horse trainer..." She picked up her empty glass and set it beside the plates, but before she could grab Jace's glass, he snatched it up. "I'm not done with my drink. Syd, what in the world are you doing?"

She looked into his eyes of concern and gave her head a hard shake. "Sorry. Sometimes when I'm stressed, I become obsessive-compulsive and need to have things symmetrically balanced. It's behaved all weekend until now."

He set down the glass and covered her hand with his. "I was worried there for a minute. You okay now?"

She nodded.

"All right. Well, I don't know everything. You're still insisting there's no chance of us dating. I want to know why."

She stiffened and wrinkled her nose. "I already told you. I need to stay in Chicago. Long-distance relationships aren't the best when there's no hope for a happy ending."

He shook his head. "Not good enough, Syd. There's more."

Keep calm, make your voice light... "Nothing much else to tell."

"Even after your mom gave you her blessing to move on and be happy?"

"Keeping my dad's dream alive isn't the same as my mother bringing a new man into her life."

"Here's a hypothetical. Let's assume we date long-distance and decide to marry. We both know I'm pretty much tied to the ranch. Why can't you work on your dad's dream from there? You have e-mail, video conferencing, websites, airplanes to bring you to Chicago if you're needed. People do it all the time for work."

Sydney surveyed the restaurant, her eyes darting from the empty booths to the lunch counter where a man sat hunched over his coffee near the hostess station in the far corner. She brought her gaze back to Jace's intense expression. "As you know, my dad's law practice was at the same firm I work for now. It's important to me to physically be there." Her excuses were sounding worse and worse. Four more hours. That's all she needed.

He released her hand and raised his hands in surrender. "I give up. Let's get going."

23

Jace buckled himself in and glanced at Sydney. She sat in the driver's seat with her hand on the ignition key. A few moments passed with no change. "Syd, is everything okay?"

She started the engine. "I was trying to come up with words that would help you understand." She faced him. Moisture glinted on her lashes in the soft glow of the mercury light above the car.

Jace's stomach knotted. He shouldn't have pushed her. He had to let it go. "I have to respect your reasons, even if I don't understand."

"Thank you." She put the car in gear and backed out of the space.

They entered the interstate and headed north. Jace slumped in his seat. His body craved sleep, but doing so would mean less time with Syd, possibly missing the last moments he'd ever have with her. He should be thinking about his brother and the mess he'd made, not how much he wanted Sydney in his life and couldn't have her. He folded his arms over his chest. There'd be plenty of time to think about Cole at the airport and during the flight, and he didn't have much time to get her talking.

"You going to be okay by yourself tomorrow?" he asked.

"I'll probably sleep in and then work on the things I didn't get done. Start Tuesday fresh."

"You didn't answer my question. Is spending tomorrow alone going to be troubling? I hate leaving you like this."

"It was more my deal than Mom's."

Evading such a question usually meant the answer was *no*. He forced his thoughts to his brother's travails to give Sydney space. The police had traced the code to his brother's laptop, but that didn't have to mean he was involved, did it? Someone could make it seem to have come from Cole's laptop. Jace knew his way around a computer, but he wasn't a techie. And like most guys Cole's age, Cole was close enough to being one. If his brother was guilty, he deserved to go to the alternative school.

Please, Lord, don't let him be guilty.

"Jace, I'm sorry for how this thing with your brother is hurting you."

Startled out of his thoughts, Jace rested his hand on her shoulder and gave it a squeeze. "I know you are. Thanks. It's not the first time I've dealt with kid-brother problems and it likely won't be the last. Time does help heal a wound."

"Sometimes a wound is so deep, time never heals it." She fell silent briefly before saying, "I need to stop for gas. I'm getting off in Champaign."

He presumed she was talking about the accidents of her brother and dad. Or was she? He only had a few more hours and was tempted to keep after the truth all the way up the interstate. He shut his eyes and prayed for patience.

Jace stirred awake, confused. The hum of tires racing over pavement told him quickly enough where he was. He should never have closed his eyes. He glanced at Sydney. She gripped the wheel with both hands with her gaze fixed on the road ahead. How long had he been asleep? He squinted at the dashboard clock. Almost one. Robbed of at least two hours.

He took a bottle of water from his backpack and opened it. After a long draw, he said, "Guess I dropped off."

Sydney lifted a juice drink to her lips and sipped as well. "No problem. I needed the time to think."

"Where are we?"

"We just passed Kankakee. It won't be long until we come to I-80 and, after that, the tollway that will take us to the airport."

He only had an hour left. He couldn't let her leave him at the curb in front of his terminal. These days, no airport let you linger longer than it took for a person to jump out and grab their gear. "When we get closer to the airport, can you get off the highway and find a place to park? I want to say good-bye without people watching us."

The last thing Syd wanted was a drawn-out good-bye, especially since she hadn't come up with a simple way of stating what she didn't want to say in the first place. Besides, lingering would only make it hurt more. But if Jace wanted a few moments, she'd somehow get through it.

She passed the airport exit and took an off-ramp into Park Ridge. After several turns, she came to a leafy residential street and parked in front of a two-story home, its darkened windows a testament to the family probably sleeping inside. "Is this okay?"

"I don't guess going to a park in the middle of the night would be too safe."

She killed the motor. "You've got that right. This may be the 'burbs, but I wouldn't chance it."

He took her hand and squeezed it. "To say I'm going to miss you, Syd, is an understatement. I already do, and we've not even said good-bye."

An ache of seismic proportions washed over her. Couldn't they just go to O'Hare and get it over with?

"Syd, say something."

"I have no words, Jace. Everything has already been said, and stretching this out isn't going to make it better."

"I know. But I can't kiss you good-bye the way I want to with the glare of airport lights everywhere."

"I'm sure the workers have seen a lot of farewell kisses."

"No doubt you're right, but I prefer it this way."

She needed to tell him the whole reason why they couldn't be together, but he'd just say it was different with him, that he'd been through the same kind of hurt and would never treat her that way. That he was truly a changed man and would never fall back on his old ways. And he'd mean it in the moment, but in the end, something would happen, and he'd have to take back his promise. It was better this way.

"I need to apologize for being so snarky with you at first about the negotiating," she said instead.

"I had it coming. And I'm sorry I messed with you just to keep you there longer."

She chuckled. "You already apologized for that. I was angry when you first told me, but I'm not anymore. I'm glad you did stall, to give us more time. I wouldn't trade these past few days for anything."

"That's encouraging." He unbuckled his seat belt, then did the same with hers and pulled her into his arms. He brought his lips to hers and feathered a kiss on them, then deepened it.

Never had she felt this way about someone, not Logan or Ryan. The kiss ended and she leaned back to look at him, wishing she could see his deep blue eyes one last time. "I have strong feelings for you and probably always will."

He pulled her close, and she pressed her face against his chest, willing the tears pushing against the backs of her eyes to subside.

"I love you, Sydney. If you ever change your mind about us, you'd better let me know."

"You love me now, but that will only last until the next woman comes along and sweeps you off your feet."

"I doubt that. But it may happen with you, Sydney. Maybe the next guy in your life will be the one to catch you off guard."

"I won't let that happen. I made my commitment to Dad's memory, and I have to keep it that way." *Safe from the unbearable pain that is sure to come.*

"Maybe it's time to let your walls down and see what happens."

"I can't, Jace."

He reached over his shoulder for his seat belt. "I can't compete with a dead man, Sydney." His buckle connected with a *snap*. "Let's head for the airport."

Sydney flinched and stared at his shadowed outline. "That hurt, Jace." She pressed the POWER button next to the steering column. The sooner he was out of her car and on his way to Texas, the better. Good thing she'd stayed strong and didn't give in. She pulled out onto the street. Tension filled the vacuum between them, so strong that she expected to see sparks in the air.

All too soon, they found the road leading to O'Hare. "American, right?"

"Yep."

She pulled to a stop in front of Terminal 3. Jace opened the door and climbed out. He reached behind the seat for his hat. "I'll get my things out of the hatch, and you can be on your way." He straightened, then leaned into the car and paused.

Was he going to apologize?

"Good-bye, Syd. Thanks for the ride."

The door slammed behind him, and after he gathered his duffel and backpack from the rear of the car, he strode to the terminal. The glass doors opened and swallowed him. Sydney strained to see through the large windows, but no one wearing a Stetson materialized.

A loud rap came at the back passenger window and she jumped. A uniformed man hunched down and shouted through the glass, "Time to be on your way."

Sydney put the car in gear and eased into the sparse traffic. She'd made the right decision, yet it felt as if half her heart was on the way to Texas. Tuesday couldn't come fast enough. Once she was back at work, the past week would fade into her memory bank and she'd be fine.

24

Jace tossed his gear into the silver Ford F-150's truck bed, then climbed into the passenger seat. His brother Tanner sat behind the wheel. "Thanks for picking me up so early."

Tanner shrugged. "You know I'm always up by now. I left the feeding to Cole. It'll do him good to work since he's confined to the ranch all week. He's lucky they let him go on his own recognizance and assurance from Mom that she'd make sure he didn't leave the ranch."

Jace sank deeper into the seat under the weight he'd carried since Mom's call yesterday, adding to the pain that hadn't left his gut since Sydney'd dropped him off at the airport. He'd not been able to shake off the regret of his last words to her. He'd hurried back outside to apologize, only to see her car pulling away. After he was certain she was off the road, he'd tried calling her, but she didn't pick up—nor did she respond to his voice mail. He brought his thoughts back to the present and glanced at Tanner. "I thought the matter was still under investigation."

Tanner pulled into traffic leaving the airport. "It is, but I don't think they have enough to charge him despite how the hack seemed to come from his computer. There are ways to spoof stuff like that, and they need more evidence. I warned him that he was getting in with the wrong crowd."

Jace frowned. "Are the guys who let air out of the bus tires techies?"

"Nah. That's another crowd. Those tech guys are arrogant, thinking they're so powerful and can hack into anyone's computer. Today, the school's servers and student laptops, and tomorrow, the White House." Tanner turned onto the main road.

"Do you think he's guilty?"

"My twin radar says he doesn't have it in him to make that kind of trouble. He's not lying. I can see it in his eyes."

"I've never known your twin radar to fail. What about the spoofing theory you mentioned?"

"The cops have this high-ranking tech specialist from the Texas Rangers on the case. He's looking into it. Meanwhile, Cole's suspended from school for the week, at least. Mom's talking about homeschooling if he's assigned to the alternative school. You know what a bad scene that place is."

"When I was in school, no one wanted to get in so much trouble that they'd end up there. Guess it hasn't changed. I'll talk to Cole when we get home."

"How's Clint? That must have been some wreck."

"He got a punctured lung and a broken leg out of it but is recovering faster than the doctor expected. I have to fly back up on Wednesday or Thursday and drive him and the rig home. He won't be much use on the ranch for a while."

"Glad it wasn't worse. Another thing. There's a fat envelope on your desk from the IRS."

"Mom told me. If it required my attention right away, Taggart would have called. I've got one of his partners working with Frisky's now to settle the contract."

"Are you sure he's the best attorney for this, Jace?"

"Why?"

"A guy on the rodeo team at school told me his dad was in the same predicament with some property he inherited, and their attorney had the problem fixed within six months."

"There're a lot of things to consider, Tanner. His could have been a totally different situation. Taggart specializes in this kind of thing for our type of property."

When they pulled onto the ranch, Cole was walking from the barn to the house, wearing a T-shirt and jeans. He glanced toward the truck and picked up his stride.

As the truck rolled to a stop, Jace leaped out and chased after him. "Cole, wait."

His brother turned, his tall, lanky body rigid with a fist on one hip. "Why? To get reamed out?"

"Not unless you deserve it. As soon as I settle in, I want us to take a ride— just the two of us—and talk it out."

Cole lifted his Stetson and ran a hand over his cropped dark hair before setting the hat back on his head. "Okay, but you didn't need to fly down here because of me. I didn't do it."

"Go get your horse and Rocky saddled up. I'll be out in a few minutes."

Tanner walked up with Jace's bags and Jace took the duffel from him. "How are you and Cole getting along since all this happened?"

"Okay. We just don't talk about it."

The back door slammed and Jace turned.

Carolyn McGowan came down the walk wearing a plaid shirt and jeans, her gray hair tied in a ponytail at her neck. Worry had replaced the usual twinkle in her eyes. "Jace, thanks for coming. I'm so sorry you had to leave Clint."

He closed the space between them and drew her into a hug. "I'm sorrier for what you've had to go through here. Clint will be okay. Lacy's with him."

"When do you have to go back north to bring him home?"

"Wednesday or Thursday. Lacy will ride back with us, since the guy who drove her and Shiloh up to the rodeo needed to leave right away."

They approached the sprawling home's back porch and stepped into the mudroom. Jace then followed his mom and Tanner into the large kitchen. "I'd say it feels good to be home, but not so much under the circumstances. I'm taking Cole out for a ride and some man-to-man conversation. Is there anything I don't know that I should?"

Tanner picked up Jace's backpack and duffel from where they'd been dropped onto the wooden plank floor. "I'll take your things to your room."

Mom pulled out a chair at the round oak table. "Let's sit for a minute."

Jace nodded and sat across from her. "We can't talk long. I've got Cole saddling the horses." He studied his mom's face. Dark shadows underscored her blue eyes—shadows that weren't there when he left.

"There's not much else to tell other than what I said on the phone. The attorney says the Rangers have one of the best men in the state working on the tech end of it, and he's sure it will prove that Cole wasn't the culprit. He's not a bad kid, Jace. The prank they pulled last week with the buses was nothing compared to this, just typical senioritis kind of stuff."

"Who's the attorney? Neal Jamison?"

"No. He recommended Seth Amphlett. He's about your age, I would guess. Understands computers and everything related. Cole likes him. I'm thinking about homeschooling Cole even if they don't charge him. School and ranch work will help keep him from mixing with the bad crowd."

"It's his senior year. He'll miss a lot."

"I know, but if he's found guilty, he'll miss everything. Either way, he'll lose. And if he's tried as an adult, it could mean..." She blinked back the tears filling her eyes. "Prison."

Jace winced and stood. Mom rose to her feet too, and he gathered her into his arms. He'd been home no more than a half hour, and already the heaviness he'd felt since yesterday had increased. "I'm gonna change clothes. I've been in these since yesterday afternoon."

Mom stood back and looked up at him. "I assume you've been awake for most of the night. Maybe you can grab a nap after your ride."

"I need to look at the IRS letter first."

The corners of her mouth turned down. "I wish they'd leave us alone. We're paying what we can."

"Lacy called after last night's rodeo and said I won the all-around. That, coupled with the money my bulls earned, means I'll be picking up a good-sized check when I fly back up. With my win, I have a spot in the NFR and hopefully will place there in my events. Things will work out."

Jace suggested to Cole that they take the trail toward the river that ran through the property. They rode side by side, letting the horses have their heads. Jace stared up at the deep blue sky. He removed his hat and wiped his brow with his forearm. Good thing he'd followed Cole's lead and worn a T-shirt instead of one of his usual long-sleeved shirts. The temperature had to be in the mid-nineties.

Even before calling his attorney, he needed to call Syd. Although he'd apologized to her in the voice mail he'd left, he longed to hear her voice and know she'd accepted it. He supposed his anger was justified at least a little, but not to the extent he'd carried it through. Leaving the way he had was not how he wanted their parting to happen, and until he righted things, the sour feeling in his stomach wasn't going away.

"What did you want to talk about?"

Jace jolted out of his thoughts and twisted in the saddle to look at his brother. "I thought we could stop by the river. Okay with you?"

"Guess so. What's with you, bro? I asked three times if you were ready to talk, and you looked like your head was a million miles from here."

"Nothin'."

"Could've fooled me. You meet some girl up there at the rodeo?"

How could his brother be so smart and so dumb at the same time? "I'm always meeting girls at rodeos. You know how it goes."

"The look on your face was different from how it usually looks after a rodeo."

"Yeah? How so?"

"I dunno. A long way from here."

Jace hoped he wasn't acting like some loony high-school kid. "How do you know so much about girls? I've never known you to have more than a couple of dates for the dances."

"I have friends."

They arrived at the river, and Jace led Cole to a spot under a sprawling oak tree. From his saddlebag, he pulled out a couple of soft drinks he'd grabbed at the house and tossed a Dr Pepper to Cole. He sat and leaned against the tree trunk, and Cole followed. Together they popped the tops on their cans and took long draws.

"So," Jace said, "why don't you start at the beginning of this hacking thing?"

"You don't want to talk about the bus deal first?"

"Later. This hacking thing is way more important."

"I had no idea what had happened until a Ranger showed up with a warrant for my laptop. Mom got all riled up and insisted I have a lawyer present, so we called Neal Jamison and he suggested Seth Amphlett. We met the Ranger at Seth's office. He said the tech guy at the high school claims he traced the breach to my computer. I wouldn't be surprised if he did it himself."

Jace frowned and stared at the can in his hands. "Why would the tech guy at school blame you?"

"He's never liked me much. I have no idea why. I only have contact with him when he comes to a classroom to fix something. It sucks that you felt you had to fly home when Clint's so banged up."

"If you could have heard Mom on the phone when she called yesterday, you'd understand. Dad's death has been hard on all of us. I'm sure she kept thinking that if only Dad were still alive, he'd know how to handle this. She looks to me to be the father figure to you guys."

"You shouldn't have to deal with this. I'm good to handle it on my own."

"Not while you're a minor. That's how it is for now. I believe you, Cole. And I hope you learned your lesson from that prank you pulled with the buses."

"Mom wants to homeschool me." Cole wrapped his arms around himself and hunched over. "I don't want to miss my senior year. I'm sending out college apps already, and it's going to look weird if I'm suddenly homeschooled."

"Have you prayed about this?"

The boy shrugged. "Not really. Praying is your thing, not mine."

Jace worked to not show his disappointment. He'd given each of the twins a Bible and talked to them about God, hoping that the way he'd changed for the good would encourage them. He needed to pray more for them and have more one-on-one talks. "Then let's pray together before we head back."

Cole nodded and bowed his head, and Jace did the same.

"Father God, you know the situation and every detail..."

Jace said "Amen" a few minutes later and raised his head. "Let's go. I need some sack time."

25

One Month Later

Sydney spotted Erin sitting in the outdoor area of their favorite lunch spot and wove between the tables toward her friend. Already the first week in October and with the days getting cooler, soon they would have to start eating their lunches inside. She slid into a chair across from Erin. "Before I even say hello, I need to apologize for not having returned those clothes you loaned me. They've been washed and are sitting neatly folded on the bench by my door. But do I remember to bring them with me to work? No."

Erin laughed. "No problem. If I need them, I know where they are."

They gave their orders to the waiter, and after he left, Erin locked her gaze on Sydney. "Okay, Syd. Fess up. You haven't returned the rodeo clothes because you keep hoping for an invitation to Texas. You know if you go, you'll need them."

Sydney grimaced as a familiar ache swelled her chest. The same ache that had been with her since she'd taken Jace to O'Hare almost a month earlier. At first she'd been angry with him, but by the time she got home, the anger had morphed into gut-wrenching pain. She'd secluded herself, except for work, during that whole week, not returning Erin's calls until the following weekend. "Erin, I told you…"

"You said you didn't want to talk about Jace. Did I mention his name?" She quirked her head and smirked. "I only said *Texas.*"

"You know he's the only person I know who lives in Texas." Sydney averted her gaze and blinked at a tear that threatened to break loose and trail down her cheek.

"Maybe if you'd tell me what happened, I'd know what to say and what not to say."

Erin was right. They'd been friends for too long for Sydney to shut her out. "I'm sorry. It's just that it's hard for me to talk about it."

"*Not* talking about him hasn't made the pain go away, has it?" Erin reached over the table for Sydney's hand. "Girlfriend, I haven't missed the pain in your eyes every time I've seen you since you got back. He must have hurt you badly. Couldn't he have let you down easy?"

"It wasn't him. It was me."

"You?"

"I always thought it would be easier to be the dumper rather than the dumpee. It's not."

The server walked up and set their lunches in front of them. "Here you go, ladies. Cobb salad for both. Can I refresh your iced teas?"

After the waiter left, Sydney picked up her fork and speared an egg white.

"Don't you want to say a blessing?"

"I already did, silently." Sydney ignored Erin's skeptical look and brought the egg white to her mouth. She paused with the fork in front of her, unable to ignore her friend's penetrating stare. "What?"

"What you said before the server brought our salads. If it was you who cut things off with Jace ... what happened?"

Sydney shrugged. "I'm not cut out for marriage. It's better to end the relationship now before it progresses to something serious. Can we just leave it at that?" She shoved the egg white into her mouth.

"How can you expect me to not ask a single question? What do you mean, you're not cut out for marriage?"

Sydney focused on the crowd moving along the sidewalk across the street. Her gaze lifted to a restaurant sign on one of the buildings. Was it only a little more than a month ago that she was at Malnati's with Jace? It seemed like an eternity. She'd been so indifferent to him that day, yet he'd stayed true to who he was then.

"Sydney, spill."

"I can't talk about it. Not here."

Erin shook her head. "Now you've got me thinking all kinds of strange thoughts. I'll be over tonight at seven. We'll talk then."

"I don't suppose it would do any good not to let you in." Sydney picked up her iced tea and gulped half of it down. They may talk, but she'd decide the topic.

Sydney's apartment buzzer sounded at seven on the dot. She hit the button to release the downstairs lock for Erin. All afternoon she'd deliberated with herself at how much she was willing to divulge to satisfy Erin's curiosity and still hadn't come to a conclusion. Truth be told, she yearned to talk to someone, and her sensibilities told her that Erin was the one person who would listen without being judgmental.

A soft knock came at the door and Sydney opened it. Wearing jeans and a jewel-toned knit top, Erin stepped inside, her curtain of strawberry-blond hair brushing her shoulders with each jaunty step as she crossed to the couch and sat.

Sydney indicated a shopping bag sitting next to the door on a small bench. "Your clothes. Thanks for loaning them."

Erin kept her gaze on Sydney and patted the cushion next to her. "Sit. You know why I'm here, and it's not to pick up my clothes."

"You want something to drink?"

"No. I want to know what's going on."

Sydney dropped to the couch and curled up in the corner opposite her friend. "I guess it's no surprise to you that I've felt miserable ever since I got home from the rodeo." She picked up her cell phone from the coffee table and found Jace's text messages. "I already told you he had to fly home on Labor Day for a family problem." She scrolled backward through the text messages. "He left a voice mail on Labor Day after he got home, saying he was sorry for upsetting me before he left. And when I didn't call back, he sent a text."

She handed Erin the phone. "You read it and the others that followed. I can't, without tearing up."

Erin took the phone and read the screen, then scrolled through the rest of Jace's texts. She looked up. "There are five or six messages here, but I don't see any responses from you. Did you e-mail or call him instead?"

Sydney shook her head as a sob worked its way out of her throat. "I keep thinking that if I don't answer, he'll give up and stop. He's also left several voice mails."

Erin returned the phone to the coffee table and frowned. "This comes close to stalking. What did he do to you, Syd? If he assaulted you, you need to report him."

Sydney gasped and grabbed Erin's arm. "No. No. Please don't think Jace would ever do anything like that. No stalking at all. He told me he loved me before I dropped him off at the airport. I've been telling myself I don't love him, don't want him in my life, but as crazy as it sounds, I ... I think I love him too."

Erin leaped up and wrapped Sydney in a hug. "Sydney, that's wonderful! I'm so happy for you."

Sydney pushed her away. "It's not wonderful, Erin. He thinks he loves me right now, but soon that feeling will fade and a cute barrel racer will come along and I'll be history."

Erin's brows arched. "Where are these thoughts coming from?"

"Don't forget, you said yourself he's a player. Erin, I've been down this road before. I know what it's like."

"I thought he said that was rumor without substantiation."

171

"He did say that, but would he admit it if he's trying to impress me? I've been fooled twice now, believing it when a man says he loves me. I'll not fall for that again—not ever."

"So you didn't tell him you loved him too?"

"I wanted to tell him, but I said what I had been saying all weekend, that I had to stay in Chicago to carry on my dad's dream. That's when he said…" She sucked in a gulp of air and let it out. "He couldn't compete with a dead man." Sydney slid to the floor and drew her knees to her chest and sobbed. "Those words sounded so hateful. I couldn't wait to get him to the airport and out of my car." She turned and looked up at Erin's stricken face. "I was angry then, but later I calmed down and began seeing it from his perspective. I must have said Dad's dream was now my dream at least a dozen times those three or four days we were together."

Erin dropped to her knees next to Sydney and wrapped her arms around her. "It's okay, sweetie. We can talk this through. Is your fear of him cheating on you the only reason you're afraid of loving Jace?"

"Isn't that enough? Think about it. I've lost everyone I've ever loved. I may as well have lost my brother. Dad died when I was sixteen, Logan left me for someone else, and Ryan went back to his former girlfriend on the day of our wedding."

Erin held up a hand. "Wait. I knew about Ryan, of course, but who is Logan?"

"A guy I seriously dated my first year of law school. We weren't yet engaged but were talking about marriage until I found out he was cheating on me.

"I felt as if a knife had been thrust into my stomach and someone was twisting it. The same way I felt when Ryan canceled our wedding." Sydney gasped for breath. "Jace is right for me in every way, but I c–c–can't go through that pain again. I already have fears that a former girlfriend will show up or a rodeo groupie will catch his eye and the same thing will happen."

Erin hugged Sydney tighter. "I'm sure my going on about my wedding plans these past few weeks hasn't helped. Love is a risk. But if you don't take the risk and trust God that He has yours and Jace's best interests at heart, your lives won't be what God intends for you as a couple. You say you have faith in God, Syd, but faith is trusting Him."

Sydney blew her nose. She hadn't thought of it from that perspective. Had she let her fears keep her from fully trusting God? A verse she'd memorized as a child came to mind. *Trust in the LORD with all your heart and lean not on your own understanding; in all your ways submit to him, and he will make your paths straight.*

She was leaning on her own understanding and not on God and His wisdom.

She faced Erin. "Jace has said more than once that God has changed him and he's a different man now. I've been thinking he is too good to be true. I've been an idiot."

Erin laughed. "I wouldn't go that far. Let's just say you've been a little misguided. I like to think He kept you from marrying anyone else until Jace came to faith, making him exactly right for you."

"But why all the pain? I've had so much."

"I know you have, sweetie. But God never said that when we begin to follow Him, life will be a bed of roses. Didn't you tell me that after your wedding was canceled you never felt closer to God than at that time?"

Sydney nodded. "Yes. The Bible's words came alive to me as never before. Then I got wrapped up in my work, and my time with the Lord became less and less." She looked at Erin. "Will you pray with me? I've got some confessing and praying to do."

26

Jace grabbed a shavings fork and began sifting the straw in Charley's stall, dumping the droppings into a nearby wheelbarrow.

"Hey, Jace, you going to be around when I get back from town?"

Jace turned and looked at Lacy, who stood in the barn door. She'd changed from the muddy jeans and work shirt she'd had on earlier into those short pants he'd heard his mother and Lacy call *capris*. The boots were gone too, replaced by a pair of sandals. "When will that be?"

"About an hour and a half. There's something I want to talk to you about, but I have an appointment soon."

"Another one of those mini-pedi things you're always getting? Yeah, I'll be here."

She laughed. "It's *mani*, not *mini*. Don't make fun of girly stuff. One of these days, some gal is going to knock you for a loop and you won't mind payin' to get her hair and nails done up."

"I doubt that." *The only gal who could knock me for a loop already has, and I can't have her.*

Lacy left the barn, and her SUV's tires crunched over the gravel and faded as she headed for the road. Jace picked up the shovel and returned to sifting the straw in Charley's stall. Ever since they'd returned from the rodeo in Illinois, Lacy had started looking more like a girl and less like a tomboy. Although she hadn't said anything, he suspected there might be a man in her life, but for the life of him, he couldn't figure out who the guy might be. If it were true, good for Lacy. He hoped she was better at love than he was. A visual of Syd emerged in his thoughts, like it did several times a day. He imagined she was back from her lunch break and working at her desk, doing more research or maybe working on the case Uncle Harry had promised to assign.

He'd cleaned several more stalls and was on the last one when he checked the time on his phone. Lacy had better be showing up soon, or he'd be out working with the cattle several miles away.

"Sorry you have to do all the work on account of me."

He turned.

Clint stood a short distance away, wearing khaki shorts and a Dallas Cowboys T-shirt. He leaned on his crutches, his leg secure in its walking cast, and smirked as he always did when ribbing Jace. He'd gotten his hair cut a few weeks ago and it no longer fell in his face.

"I'll get you back when you heal, buddy. Meanwhile, it's my pleasure. Keeps me humble while you get all fat and sassy, lying around."

"Trust me, I'd rather be mucking stalls than doing what I'm doing. I'm even watching soap operas. That ought to tell you how bad it is."

Jace threw his head back in laughter. "Looks like I've gotta come up with something to keep you occupied, if it's come to that. Can't have you getting all soft on me."

Clint looked at his watch. "Lacy should be back anytime now."

Was something going on between him and Lacy? "Missing her, huh?"

"Yeah. Kind of. She's a nice girl."

"Well, that cousin of mine had better show up soon. I'm fixin' to head out to check on the herd."

"I wouldn't leave just yet if I were you."

Jace frowned. "She told me to stay here before she left. She'd better not be pulling one of her 'surprises' on me." His birthday wasn't for another month. Whatever she was up to, it didn't sound good. He had half a mind to disappear.

Clint smiled. "I think I hear her now."

The faint sound of tires on gravel grew louder. Jace ran the shavings fork through the straw one last time as the crunching sound halted nearby.

Lacy appeared in the doorway of the barn with her face flushed and looked at Jace. "Good. You're still here."

"I said I would be."

"Well, then, come on outside."

He trudged past Clint, who was tugging his phone from his jeans pocket. Lacy had her phone in her hand. Something weird was going on. He stepped into the bright sun and looked around. Nothing seemed out of the ordinary.

Then he saw her.

His breath hitched.

He wasn't dreaming.

There she was in the flesh, looking mighty fine in jeans, boots, and a pink shirt with sparkly things on it. Her blond waves framed her beautiful face, and she was smiling that smile that always took his breath away.

"Sydney, what are you doing here?"

She stepped closer. "I'm here to tell you that I was wrong, especially about our not being together. I'm sorry for putting you through the wringer because of my hang-ups." Her lower lip trembled. "I wanted to tell you in person that God has shown me I have to be willing to take a risk on us and trust Him for my future—our future."

Jace's pulse ramped up as her words sank in. He looked at the wheeled suitcase Lacy had just retrieved from her car. "By the size of your suitcase, it doesn't look like you plan to stay long."

She stepped a little closer. "I have two weeks off and can stay the whole time—with plans to come back for good, if you'll have me."

"What about your dad's dream?"

"I'm still on the board of directors at VLA and will have to attend the annual meeting, but that's all. There's a place near Chicago where I can become certified as a therapeutic horse trainer ... but there's also one here in San Antonio." She raised her brows and offered a questioning gaze.

He started walking and didn't stop until he could look down into those deep pools of chocolate-brown eyes and inhale her flowery scent. "You'd better not be kidding, Sydney Knight."

Moisture glinted on her eyelashes, and she blinked. "I'm not kidding, Jace. I love you, and I hope you still feel the same about me."

He ran his gaze over her face, then kissed away a tear that trailed down her cheek. "Every day we've been apart, I haven't stopped loving you. In fact, I love you more than ever."

"Then are you saying I made the right decision to come?" She encircled his waist with her arms.

"I smell like a barn. I'm not sure you want to do that until I catch a shower."

She rose on her tiptoes. "You smell just fine to me, cowboy."

His lips found hers. Soft, tender, and finally where they belonged. He leaned back and looked into her eyes. "Does that answer your question?"

Cheers erupted behind them, and they stepped apart. Clint held up his cell phone. "Got a great video. How 'bout you, Lacy?"

She grinned. "Yep, mine's good. I'll get it up on Facebook as soon as I get inside."

Jace shook his head and grinned. "Don't you need our permission before you do that?"

"Don't you want the world to know that this story has a happy ending?"

Jace laughed at his cousin, then looked at Sydney. "You okay with that?"

"May as well let all the buckle bunnies know you're taken."

"And happily so." He kissed her again. "I wouldn't want to belong to anyone but you."

Epilogue

Eight Months Later

Sydney stood in the ranch's guestroom—her room since she'd permanently moved to Texas four months earlier, after she'd resigned from the law firm and sold her condo. The time wasn't all business while she was in Chicago. She'd flown to Vegas in December to watch Jace compete in the National Finals Rodeo and win first place in the overall bull riding average. His winnings were enough to pay off the balance of the taxes and complete the building of his house. As of today, their house.

Jace had insisted on coming to Chicago over the Christmas holidays to meet her mom, stepdad, and brother. She soon realized after observing her stepdad and mom together that they really *were* good for each other. Russ would never replace the memory of Dad—no one could do that. But when it came time to decide who would accompany her down the aisle, she had a difficult time deciding between Russ and Nate. She'd made the right decision in choosing Nate, but Russ would take the place of her dad for the father-daughter dance.

"One more pull and we're done." Erin tugged at the dress's corset laces. "Take a deep breath."

Sydney snapped out of her reverie and did as she was told, holding the breath she took.

"Done. Now step across the room so I can see how it looks from the front."

"All I can say is, I'm sure glad we don't live in the nineteenth century when corsets were a must-have." Sydney crossed the room and turned. Erin's smile said it all.

"Beautiful, Syd. It fits you perfectly."

She stepped over to the full-length mirror and peered at her reflection. The woman staring back was the person she never thought she'd become. But God had other plans, and here she was about to marry her best friend and the only man God had in mind for her years before she realized it.

She ran her palms down the lacy bodice. The way she'd been taste-testing reception food during the past few weeks and eating her way through three wedding showers and last night's scrumptious rehearsal dinner barbeque, she wasn't sure if the dress would still fit.

She loved how the layers of taffeta in the skirt captured the country look she was after. She lifted the skirt to reveal polished brown boots. The dozen pairs of stilettos she owned were sitting in the master bedroom closet at the new house, along with the rest of her clothes that were moved over there yesterday. Would she ever wear those shoes again? Probably not, but it was still too soon to say never.

She touched her fingertips to the red roses and baby's breath artfully arranged in her hair. She loved how Lacy's stylist had left some loose curls out of the twist at the back of her head to softly frame her face the way Jace loved.

Erin came up next to her, wearing an off-white, shabby-chic-style, knee-length dress and boots. "You are a gorgeous bride."

Sydney hugged her friend. "As you were last month. Thanks for being my matron of honor."

"I wouldn't miss your wedding. Of course, I'm very jealous of your living on a ranch and riding horses every day."

"You can visit whenever you like. We can always use more help around here."

"It's time, ladies." Lacy strolled in wearing a dress identical to Erin's, as the only other bridesmaid. "The musicians have started, and Jace is looking mighty nervous."

"He's not already up front, is he?" Sydney glanced at the bedroom clock. Five minutes before wedding time.

"No. I spotted him hiding out at the side of the barn—pacing. Clint and the twins are talking to him. He'll be okay."

Sydney could imagine that conversation. In the four months she'd been on the ranch, she couldn't miss how much the twins loved and looked up to Jace. Never were they so grateful that the culprit who'd made the hack job look as if Cole had done it was caught. As suspected, it was the IT guy on staff who was now doing time.

The women walked together through the back door and across the lawn toward what used to be the ranch's main barn. Now used for storage, the structure had been cleaned out and put to a new use for the wedding. Most of the quilt-covered hay bales were filled with their guests, while the twins, serving as ushers, led a few guests to the remaining seats. Sydney scanned the crowd. There were Harry and his wife, along with a few of their colleagues from the law office. She'd expected Jace's uncle and aunt to make the trip from Chicago, but not the other two guys. In front of them were Corey's wife Molly with their two children.

"Is someone making sure Jace doesn't come around the barn until it's time?" she asked. "I don't want him seeing me until I start down the aisle."

"Pastor Warren and the groomsmen won't let it happen. No worries." Lacy smoothed Sydney's skirt. "What a perfect day. Much better than yesterday's rain."

They reached the makeshift aisle that led to where she and Jace would exchange vows in front of the fancied-up barn door. She hadn't known whether her brother would be able to give her away, given the difficulty he had with travel. But here Nate was, rolling up the aisle to meet her. She returned his grin and waved from her position out of view of the guests. "You ready?"

"You bet, sis." His face grew serious. "We haven't had much of a chance to talk since I arrived so late yesterday, but I want to say that I am very honored you asked me to give you away. I've given you a rough time and took out my frustration on you. I'm sorry."

Sydney's heart felt as if it was going to explode. She bent and wrapped her arms around him. "No worries. I love you, Nate."

"I love you too, sis."

Sydney straightened and was dabbing at the moisture rimming her lower eyelids when one of Jace's aunts rushed up and handed her the sunflower-and-red-rose bouquet Sydney and Jace had designed together. The roses were her choice, and the sunflowers were his.

Erin and Lacy, carrying smaller bouquets of sunflowers and baby's breath, stepped around Sydney and approached Nate, as the musicians switched gears and began a song more befitting a processional.

Pastor Warren came around the corner of the barn, followed by Jace—who was wearing a black Stetson, a white vest and tie, pressed black jeans, and a black jacket. Sydney's heart raced. He looked beyond handsome. God had blessed her so much, and she deserved so little.

Clint and Corey followed the groom, wearing black jeans and boots, dark brown vests over long-sleeved shirts, and white Stetsons. They too looked handsome, but Sydney only had eyes for Jace.

Lacy started down the aisle, followed by Erin. When they reached the others at the front, Sydney stepped out of the shadows and came up beside Nate. She held her bouquet in her left hand and rested her right hand on Nate's shoulder. "Ready when you are."

The guests stood according to the music, and Sydney let her brother set the pace with his electric chair while she walked beside him over the wooden planks laid down for the wheelchair. Her eyes met Jace's, and she giggled at his huge grin. As she neared him, he mouthed, "I love you." Finally she was next to him. Jace whispered his thanks to Nate, and her brother inched his chair backward to the end of the first row of seats, next to their mom and stepdad.

Jace took her hand and squeezed it. "My most beautiful bride," he whispered.

"You're just biased."
"You bet I am. Ready to get married?"
"More than ready. Let's do it."

THE END

FOL

FEB 1 3 2024

Made in the USA
Lexington, KY
14 August 2017